Ladies and Escorts

Published by Black Moss Press, 2450 Byng Road, Windsor, Ontario, Canada
N8W 3E8.
Black Moss Press books are distributed by Firefly Books, Scarborough,
Ontario, Canada
Black Moss Press is grateful for grants from the Ontario Arts Council
and the Department of Canadian Heritage.
We acknowledge the support of the Canada Council for the Arts for our
publishing program.

ISBN 088753-301-9

Acknowledgements

A section of this book was previously published in *That Sign of Perfection*
Cover photo: Jevon Safarik
The author wishes to thank Allan Safarik for editorial assistance.

Ladies
and
Escorts

Dolores Reimer

Black Moss Press
1997

In memoriam
Herman Henry Reimer

"Scuse me ma'm. Do you have any spare change?"

The black windbreaker the woman wore was torn under each arm. Her white t-shirt was tinged gray, with dribble stains down the front. Tomato vegetable soup for lunch Fiona thought.

She knew the woman was going to ask this. She had a premonition as soon as she noticed her in the distance. It wasn't a tingle or a sudden rush of knowledge. She didn't tell herself, this woman is going to ask me for money. She just knew, the same way she knew what was going to happen in movie reruns; the same way she knew when father died, or Robert got his job, or she could feel she was in trouble.

Fiona watched her walk toward her for almost a block. She noticed the missing hand when the woman stopped in front of her. The hook that hung from the ribbed cuff of the jacket was silly putty pink. The real hand was in front of her open, palm up, slightly cupped. There was a scar, a mark from stitches running across the life line, pink like the vulnerable belly of the porcupine when it is exposed.

Fiona's mouth went dry. She looked over the woman's shoulder. The door to the bus depot was still half a block away. She started getting cramps in her stomach. Fiona turned her head furtively looking for Robert before realizing she didn't have to worry what Robert thought about it today. She wouldn't have to defend her actions or try to hide slipping the coins into the outstretched hand. She wouldn't have to endure the you're-just-as-low-as-them-for-being-so-weak-as-to-give-to-a- panhandler stare Robert would always give her. He walked by. Eyes ahead. Face stone cold. He never gave anything. Ever. Not even a look in the eye.

"They'll just spend it on booze."

"Some of these people are richer than we'll ever be."

This was two of the ways he began his lecture. He'd end with, "The least you could do is pick one registered charity to give to each year and get a tax receipt." She never listened to the in between.

Fiona always gave. All her change. Bills even, the smaller ones. Robert never understood. For years she tried to explain her reason but nothing she said made an impact or dent in his opinion.

"Remember the fairy tale about the pitcher of milk that never ran out?"

Robert gave her a wary look.

"Well," Fiona went on, "There was a poor couple living in the forest.

They were poorer than the poorest person ever could be. One day two travellers arrived on their door step. They fed the travellers from their larder as best they could, and treated them as kings. The travellers, unknown to their host and hostess, were endowed with magical powers and rewarded the couple with a jug of milk that continuously filled itself. The moral of the story being that you never know when the Gods are testing you."

"Testing, Fiona?" Robert rolled his eyes.

"Yes. Testing your good will toward mankind. Will you be rewarded for treating people as kings? Or will a black mark go on your record book because you ignore people in need?"

"There but for the grace of God." Father always said to Fiona pointing with his chin at the panhandlers after he emptied his pockets of change.

"You never know when fortune turns. Disaster could strike tomorrow and you'd have to depend on the good graces of others." He'd reach into his jangly pocket to bringing out a handful of change. He would look at the coins, shake them a bit in his closed hand, the way they shook the dice playing monopoly, then he passed them to the other person saying things like, "And a good day to you sir." Or he would shake their hand and talk about the weather.

Robert shook his head. "Why do you have to justify wasting money in such a manner?"

She couldn't tell him. Sometimes the beggars reminded her of father; the ragged clothes, desperate eyes, unwashed hair, the smell of stale alcohol, and the racking cough. She knew there would be disdain in his eyes if she ever confessed this secret. Robert knew there was something she wasn't telling him. That's why he always asked her the justify question. The challenge was in his eyes bright and knowledgeable like a curious animal. Fiona figured he'd already guessed and was waiting for her to tell him. Waiting the way a cats waits for a mouse to make the wrong move. Patient, ready to pounce.

The last time she saw father he was living on skid row in Calgary. Robert's vision of the ideal life didn't include a father-in-law like Peter. This was one bum he couldn't ignore as he crossed the street, one outcast from society he had to shake hands with in public.

Today she didn't have to worry about justification for anything she did. Robert was in Saskatoon and she was in Vancouver. The tenseness left her shoulders.

Fiona smiled at the woman. She took a twenty out of her wallet and handed it over. The woman grinned back at her.

"If you're tallying points God," she said outloud, "give that one to father."

Everything in Vancouver was magnified. The highrises were taller, the crowds were larger, traffic was noisier, the rich were richer, the poor poorer. The poor people in Vancouver had better winters than the ones in Saskatoon, thought Fiona as she opened the door to the bus depot and walked into the melee of people coming and going. She stood for a moment to get her bearings and read the signs, then made her way through the rest of the building slowly.

"Twenty-four hours Vancouver to Saskatoon." The ticket agent told her when she paid her fare. As she made her way to the departure gate she was careful not to meet anyone's eyes. Bus stations are bad for chatty travellers she thought as she stood in line waiting to board the bus. Being aloof and unfriendly was some insurance that she wouldn't get stuck sitting with an incessant talker; someone who wouldn't let her read her books, or someone who talked too loud and let everyone on the bus listen to their conversation.

Once she was on board she had to wait at the front of the bus for the woman two ahead of her to settle into the front seat. She tried to look down the crowded bus to see if there was a seat she could claim. If she was lucky there would still be an empty one and she could sit next to the window, if not she would have to do a quick inspection of the seated passengers to determine who was the least threatening. These situations made her uncomfortable, it was such a gamble, like grab bags at a rummage sale.

Strange, Fiona thought, the way the reflection in the windows of the woman ahead of her reminded her so much of mother. It was eerie, the slope of the shoulders, the shape of the head, the rhythm of the walk...all instantly recognizable, ingrained into her head from many years of watching her mother's movements. The clothes were a little different than what mother would wear, but it was so uncanny. She found an empty window seat and took her place. It was then, as the reflection followed her into the bus seat she realized it was herself. The disorientation of time and space and travel played tricks on her. Then mortification took over. How could this be?

"You're just like your mother!" Father was laying on the couch watching football one Saturday afternoon. He laughed and took a long drink of his beer, emptied the bottle, chuckled as he opened another.

Fiona was burning. She could feel the red in her cheeks, the tightening of her facial muscles, the searing pain in her stomach, the explosion in her chest. Rage made her clench her hands and curl her toes.

"I am not like my mother! I never have been and I never will be!" Fiona stomped her foot for emphasis and left. Father's laughter followed her out of the room.

Fiona's face turned red even remembering this. She couldn't say what the events were leading up to this memory, when, where, why, who knows She tried so hard not to be mother, yet there she was is in the reflection of herself. Definitely Jaqueline's daughter.

She watched the lights and the buildings out the bus window through the reflection of her face as the big vehicle rolled out of downtown Vancouver. Genetics weren't fair, God played hardball with your head-space.

Fiona thought of her neighbour, Beryl. Beryl was eighty four. When she was eighty her mother died at the grand age of 100.

"Same age difference as there is between mother and I." Fiona told her, "Just different generations." After she offered her condolences she remembered thinking...imagine living most of your life with your mother around. You'd never get a break.

When mother is ninety, and she will be ninety Fiona told herself, I'll be seventy. We'll be old gray haired ladies together, old smelly gray haired ladies and it will still matter, this mother daughter distinction will still be there. Always there would be that person who could remember the stupid things you did in life, or could reduce you to tears with a look, wither your self-confidence and remind you of your inadequacies with only a small reminder of past indiscretions; a key word, a name you've forgotten from long ago. Always she could tell the stories of the inconvenient and embarrassing places you vomited as a child. Could you ever be really totally independent while your mother was alive when you were an old woman?

Fiona leaned her head against the window. The coolness of the glass against her forehead. She tried to look into houses as the bus drove passed them, tried to peer into living room windows that still did not have the drapes closed but had a light on, or a kitchen window. Looking for what? Decorating tips only, the angle of the bus too awkward to catch lovers in an embrace or children playing. She could see the odd person doing dishes. The peeping tom furtively touching humanity.

Our Lady of Sorrows Catholic Church. Sunday Mass 10:00 she read. Light shone through the church windows. Cozy warmth on an ugly night.

Ladies and Escorts, a bright light shining through. Neon pink. The sign startled her. She missed the name of the hotel. She lifted an eyebrow in surprise. The sign in front of the Gateway Hotel was never that fancy. A yellow light like an upside down taxi light with Ladies and Escorts in serviceable black letters decorated the Gateway Hotel. She watched the neon letters as long as she could. The letters were like handwriting, loops, curves and twirls.

"Ladies and Escorts." Fiona whispered against the bus window, her warm breath fogging the glass, melding the colours of the city night making her eyes an out of focus camera as if they were full of tears. She wiped the glass with the palm of her hand and went back to looking in peoples' houses.

Her life was spent waiting for things. Long hours of nothing to do but watch. Waiting for her parents, Robert, the weather to change, the bank lineup to shrink, the clock to move its way around to where it started another day.

*   *   *

Ladies.

"You sit right there young lady and don't move." Mother lecturing about something else Fiona did wrong.

"Ladies sit with their knees together, ankles together or slightly crossed and their hands folded in their laps." Mrs. Keats the guidance counsellor in grade 6.

"Lady can you buy a box of cookies to support the girl guides?" Two of them at the door in blue uniforms.

"Hey lady!...nice shirt, if you know what I mean...heh, heh." The construction workers downtown.

" Lady, what the hell do you think your doing?" The cop writing out a ticket after she ran a red light.

*   *   *

Ladies and Escorts, yellow light, black letters.

"You can't go to the dance unless you have an escort Fiona."

Funny how a date was something you were asked out on and an escort was your responsibility to obtain. Protected. With an escort your reputation will be protected. Reputation for what? Ah mother if only you knew...if only you knew. Billy putting his hand up her shirt during the slow dances, the softness of his lips on hers, the smell of Thrills gum and vodka, the touch of his fingers brushing her nipple, the walk home past the baseball diamond, the dugout sheltered from view...protected, home on time, lips red.

"I used to be a good girl," whispered Fiona fogging the window again.

Yellow blocks, yellow sign, black letters, 36 parking meters on both sides of the street, the sparrows nesting under the HOTEL sign. Mother and father disappearing through the Ladies and Escorts door, Mr. Simpson, the school principal, through the Gentlemens' door. The heart drawn with black marker, an arrow through it on the fifth row up from the bottom beside the Ladies and Escorts entrance. Hot sweltering days in the car waiting for mother and father to come out. Drinking Cokes and reading comics all day. If it was winter she waited in the lobby. Fiona knew every cigarette burn in the multi coloured carpet. There were three doors here, one that said Office, one that said Registered Guests Only and led down the hall, one that said Beer Parlour.

Hardly anyone went through the Registered Guests Only door. Lots of people went through the Beer Parlour door. Fiona thought watching the people coming and going from the Beer Parlour was better than watching tv. Sometimes people were romantic with each other. Sometimes they were funny, telling jokes or singing funny songs, or dancing. Sometimes they were fighting. She didn't like that very much. Fiona was afraid their anger would spill over into the lobby and catch her. Her back up plan was to run and hide between the pop machine and the cigarette machine.

Once she heard father fighting with another man. They were arguing. She tried not to listen to their loud gruff voices. She could hear a woman crying. Father stomped into the lobby, looked surprised to see Fiona.

"Time to go Princess." He left in a hurry. Fiona had to run to catch up with him.

"You forgot about me didn't you?" she asked.

"Shut up Fiona before you start sounding like your mother."

Usually waiting in the lobby was boring. Long hours of clock watching, reading comic books twice. After a long Saturday of waiting for mother and father, Fiona could close her eyes and see the carpet pattern instead of the usual darkness.

"Marla, there's a new cigarette burn over by the brown chair," she said one day in wonderment. That's when Marla gave her knitting lessons.

*   *   *

"It's only a bunch of knots." Robert was unimpressed with her knitting.

"How can you sit there all night doing nothing with a piece of string?"

She pointed out she was making clothing and blankets to keep people warm. Besides they were beautiful things. Handknit. Homemade. The throw she knit for the couch was part of the decoration, adding atmosphere to their house. People were always complementing her creations.

"Yeah, if you like that cheap kind of decorating."

"Only a bunch of knots," whispered Fiona.

"Tied up in knots." She felt the bus pick up speed as it hit the highway.

"Only a piece of string that can keep you warm, only a bunch of knots holding things together..only a...only a...god it's all come unravelled! I've darned all the holes I can and now the bottom is unravelling."

*   *   *

Hands.
Then Screams.

Or was it the other way around? Screams. Then hands.

She couldn't remember. Not properly anyway. The sequence of events were a bit fuzzy around the edges. She couldn't feel anything, not relief, not panic, not thankfulness, just nothing. There was a big empty space inside. She noticed she was shaking when the woman helped her up, and she had to wipe her upper lip with the kleenex that was in her pocket. She remembered this because it was so unusual. There were times she had experienced breaking out all over in a sweat. There were times she had a dry mouth because of nervousness, but never before did sweat break out on her upper lip. Perspiration as mother called it.

"Ladies don't sweat, they perspire, or glow."

This was definitely sweat, mother. Fiona thought.

Two hours later she was still numb. The feeling stayed with her through lunch. It hung around while she ran her errands. Now she thought this was the way she was going to always be....numb...experiencing life through a long tunnel. Not a bad idea, Fiona thought, you would still feel things, but the bite would be taken out the way the dentist takes the edge off the pain. A permanent shot of novocaine for numbing the psyche.

Here she was standing on the same corner. People were going about their business, traffic was moving as it always does. The routine of downtown Saskatoon on a Wednesday afternoon in summer carried on without change. Except for her. Except for the tunnel she felt she was looking down. It was even dark around the edges the way binocular lenses were sometimes.

Standing on the corner, la la -la la la-la. Fiona sang to herself and suddenly stopped. It was still there. Still sitting in the middle of the crosswalk. Still round and bright pink, untouched by car wheels, not trod upon by someone, or stuck to a shoe and carted elsewhere.

Two hours ago she had noticed the gob of pink bubble gum. She was crossing at this same corner. The crosswalk light changed to walk. She was watching the woman on the other side of the street in the kind of outfit her mother would approve of, tailored nicely, matching shoes and handbag. She was just thinking the woman probably had a matching brief-case beside her desk in what ever downtown office she worked in when the light changed. Keeping her eyes on her she began to cross. We'll meet in the middle she was thinking when she noticed the car. A left turn on a red light. She tried to step back but slipped and fell, closed her eyes and waited.

When she opened them all she could see was the pink gum glistening against the gray pavement two inches from her face. That's when the screams and hands became confused. Just as she was wondering how anyone could put that much gum in their mouths, hands lifted her to her feet. Miss Perfect asking, "Are you alright?"

"Yes, thank-you," Fiona replied brushing off her jeans, dusty from the asphalt. Miss Perfect was ready to administer first aid.

"I think you should see a doctor."

"I'm alright. Really."

She went quickly on her way to lunch with Brenda, wiping her upper lip as she reached the other side of the street. A few people watched and then the world just kept going.

When she related the tale to Brenda, she could still picture the imprint of someone's front teeth on the gum, tiny clear bubbles of saliva all over it, gray asphalt, whitewall tires as they passed by. Brenda just shrugged her shoulders, and Fiona couldn't remember what happened at lunch after that. It was all a bit fuzzy. Like now, waiting for another light to change. This was the second time through. She couldn't bring herself to cross the street. Fiona was watching the gum the way she watched Brenda eat her lunch, twirl her hair, pick her front teeth with the nail of her baby finger, watched Brenda's red lips moving and heard her voice but nothing registered. Only black tires, white stripe, gray pavement, pink gum, a short scream, "Are you alright?"

Am I alright?

Hands lifting her off the street, Oscar De la Renta perfume. Pink bubble gum. Hands.

Don't walk is a red hand. A crowd gathered. The light turned. Everyone pressed forward. Four men in suits, two women with shopping bags, a grandmother with her children. Everyone hurrying to cross the street.

She double checked the cars; right and left. Fiona crossed with the crowd, there was safety in numbers. She bent briefly just before the other sidewalk and picked up the gob of bubblegum. It was dry. Robert would be mortified. But it didn't matter anymore. She would keep it on her dresser next to the jewelry box and the china figurine her mother-in-law gave her for Christmas two years ago. She wrapped it in a kleenex and put it in her purse. The perfect talisman for traveling, she'll tell Robert. Already tested and full of good luck. She snorted as she unlocked the car door. As if he'll like that. As if he'll care.

* * *

It didn't take much, she thought, a careless word, a criticism, a betrayal. Heartbroken, hearthurt, heartache. Robert. Sometimes the pain is too much to bear, the sharpness of it running along the arms, starting in each wrist and working its way up to the chest, two rivers of pain that meet in the heart, wondering how it can go on beating. The sudden weakness of the arms, the sudden dry mouth, the sharp prick of tears in the eyes at the same time the lightning inside strikes across the chest. The ....Oh no, the rush of feeling, the thunder inside, the roar in the ears, the shortness of breath, the inability to speak, wondering how long you must endure, ten seconds? Two hours? A day? Longer? The unfairness of the internal earthquake and destruction; the rest of the world still the same, the beauty of it unmarred, the sun still shining, or the colours of the flowers still bright, or the people at the next restaurant table still laughing, the woodgrain in the table still patterned not askew. Then the aftershocks, the waves of pain that keep coming. Wondering when it will stop. The memory of it so easy to return unexpectedly, another internal earthquake. Again the sharpness in the arms, in the heart, as if damage to the emotional heart is felt in the physical heart, wondering if she can possibly live through it.

So much easier, Fiona found, to exist in a state of emotional detachment. Somewhat like the way you had to cope with an emergency: a car accident you happen upon, lots of blood...obviously fatal, or an accidental amputation at the bus stop, a hold up at the bank, a bomb threat at the theatre, fire drill at work...hold on to yourself...keep calm. Put yourself on automatic. Don't panic. Do what has to be done as efficiently as possible. Roboworker. Be brave. Cry when you're by yourself, in the dark, in the shower, in the bath, washing dishes, changing the laundry, waiting at a red light...let loose somewhere when you're alone. Remember the sun still shines the next day and somehow, God only knows how, you wake up and find you actually did sleep. You're still alive. Roboperson.

Things still caught her unaware. No matter what the preparation. No matter how many warning signs of imminent disaster she filed in her head for later identification. Filed under headings like: MOTHER, ROBERT, WORK, FRIENDS, FATHER, FAMILY, MYSELF, the signs changed periodically, mutated the way bacteria and viruses did, hit suddenly and harshly and left her trying to hold the pieces of herself in one place while she built the wall inside that kept them all together.

Now this, another disaster, another crisis, a brush with death. Fiona drove out of the parking lot. It was a hot summer day, sunshine so bright the sky had lost its colour. So hot nothing was attractive anymore, the cement downtown, the asphalt, the flowers in such sharp relief it was all surreal.

What advice would mother have for today she wondered? What did ladies do or not do in this situation? Were there any rules? The tears rolled down her cheeks, she pulled over to the side of the road and parked. She was surprised to see her arms shaking so much, she held herself, arms crossed around her chest, hands clasping the opposite shoulders; felt the panic, the fear, and the relief she should have felt earlier all in one rush she pushed the car seat back and doubled over and cried.

*   *   *

Fiona was fumbling around in mother's hall closet. It was a week before Easter and she was helping mother do her spring cleaning. She wasn't really sure if this was what mother wanted, but she took the hint on the phone to mean she needed help so here she was burning her lungs out with cleansers and clogging her sinuses with dust. She came across a shoe box half full of father's papers; birth certificate, high school diploma, baptism certificate, an envelope with four pictures. She added a few items of father's she found around the house; a pocket watch that never worked as far as Fiona could remember, an amortization handbook with father's name in it, a pair of slippers Aunt Hilda knit for him 20 years ago, one of those pens that dressed or undressed a woman depending on the angle the pen was tilted, a royal flush poker hand tie-clip, three packages of matches from the St. Regis Hotel in Winnipeg that she found in one of his suit jacket pockets, and a green and white peter warmer the neighbour two moves ago crocheted and gave to him for Christmas the year Fiona turned 15.

Fiona sifted around the few belongings, had a look at the paper work she found, admired the fancy calligraphy and adornment on the official papers and had a look at the pictures in the envelope. She didn't think she had seen these particular ones before, but they were variations on a theme from any family album. The first picture was one of her parents. Jaqueline is enormously pregnant and Peter looks handsome and happy. They are dressed to go out for the evening. The kitchen cupboards are obviously Aunt Ethel's. There are two pictures of Fiona. One with Peter. She sits on her father's knee, enveloped in his arms. He is holding her like a fragile china doll. Fiona has dark circles underneath her eyes and her hair is matted as if she just got up. The date on the photo says August 1958. Fiona is not quite one year old. In the third picture her Aunt Monique is handing a popsicle to her across the kitchen table. Fiona must be three in this picture, because that is when Jaqueline and Monique started visiting again and then suddenly stopped. There is a bandage on Fiona's head. Aunt Monique is smiling, Fiona is not. In the last picture a young Jaqueline is sitting beside her mother on a couch. The date on the photograph reads July 1955.

The pictures are all black and white. Fiona puts them back in the envelope and drops them into the box. She jiggles the box back and forth listens to the sound this odd collection makes together and smiles.

She hears mother's voice, but is ignoring her. Jaqueline's mouth is moving, but Fiona is not listening. It is probably a further discourse on why her newest hair cut is not acceptable, or she's put something back in the wrong spot, or she left a streak on the bathroom mirror when she cleaned it.

"What have you got there?" Jaqueline asks behind Fiona.

"I don't know, a bunch of father's stuff and some pictures I've never seen before. I was just cleaning out the closet here and put together a bunch of stuff, kind of a memory box. You might want to put these pictures with the rest of the family album."

"Time for coffee." Jaqueline takes the box Fiona holds out to her, wanders into the kitchen and picks through the collection Fiona gathered. Her face grows red when she shuffles through the pictures. Slowly she tears them in quarters and throws them into the garbage.

Fiona raises her eyebrows, "Mom?"

Jaqueline's eyes fill with tears, "Can't you ever leave well enough alone? You always do this to me! Who asked you to come today anyway?"

"Lets have a coffee break."

Fiona drops used coffee grounds from the morning all over a montage of memories and history she knows nothing about. She hesitated before she did, thinking that good photography shops could repair damaged photos but mother was so upset she thought maybe an action like that would break the tension.

"Take out the garbage, get that bag out of here and go home."

*   *   *

Jaqueline watches her daughter leave.

"It's none of your goddamned business," she yells out the window as Fiona drives away.

When they were hidden in the dark Jaqueline could forget the pictures and everything about them, close the ugly parts away. Suddenly there they were, faces of the past looking up to the ceiling, let loose, filling her kitchen with shame and memories of events she had tried to pretend never happened. She wipes her eyes with a balled up kleenex, her nose on the back of her sleeve.

Jaqueline can see the green bag on the garbage stand by the alley when she looks out her bathroom window. Every morning she checks, looks past the flower beds she needs to weed; past the spruce tree she and Peter planted; hoping by some miracle the bag might magically disappear before the next scheduled garbage collection. At night in her bed she feels the hands of the past choking her. She moves to the couch in the living room. The windows here face the street not the back yard where that green bag sits, memory pointing accusing fingers at her. She spends all day at the mall wandering up and down the halls, trying on clothes she never intends to buy, takes in afternoon matinees of movies she never intended to see. She eats dinner out every night for a week just to avoid the oppression that's moved into the house. In the evening she drinks rye and coke and watches infomertials on tv until she passes out. Jaqueline puts cardboard over the bathroom window when she showers so she won't be tempted to look outside, so she won't feel the lump in her stomach when she feels the shock of setting eyes on the object that brings so much guilt.

She hears the garbage truck a week later and runs to watch out the bathroom window. She stands on the edge of the tub to get a better view. A young man throws the bag into the black mouth at the back of the garbage truck and slowly it makes its way down the alley. He throws bags from each house along the block in with hers. Other peoples' garbage covers her secrets. Soon the truck is gone. The destroyed pictures leaving only a shadow on the back of Jaqueline's mind, small and comfortable the way it was before when they were hidden in the dark.

I

Jaqueline runs down the stairs to have supper with her mother and sister. She is happy. Today is her mother's birthday. They are having the roast Jaqueline bought for the birthday dinner. It isn't everyday they've been able to have beef for dinner. For desert she bought a frosted cake from the bakery.

She feels beautiful today, a new dress and nice red lipstick on her lips. It is late spring and the sun is shining on all the trees, everything is new and growing.

Jaqueline works at the telephone company, the midnight shift, and doesn't have time to bake cakes or make supper. Part of her pay cheques supplement her mother's widow's pension. Still, she has saved half of her pay cheques for the last six months and has the kind of clothes she used to dream of owning all her life. No more hand me downs from her cousins in Ontario. She has money to be a lady like the ones she reads about in TRUE STORY magazines and HARLEQUIN ROMANCES. Jaqueline may have grown up poor but she certainly knows what quality things you need to be a lady and catch a good man to marry.

"Happy Birthday Mom!" she gives her a kiss on her left cheek and sits at the table across from her sister Monique.

"Another new dress?" her mother asks, "Too fancy to wear for a dinner at home and too fancy for you to wear to work"

The older woman shakes her head, "I've told you before, you must learn to be more practical."

"And how else am I going to catch a rich man to marry and keep you in comfort for the rest of your life?"

"What is rich anyway? Huh? A little more than we have now? A lot more than we have now? I'm comfortable just like I am. Why are you trying to be something you're not? Its just smoke and mirrors...you're just a girl from across the tracks. Stop trying to be something you're not."

Jaqueline's eyes grow cold, "Just eat dinner now Mom, we have a nice cake to celebrate."

"Not as good as home made I'll bet."

"Will you two stop it!" Monique yells, "lets have a nice homey evening."

Jaqueline keeps her head down the rest of dinner. She eats very little. How can she say that to me? How can she not like new clothes, meat for dinner more than once a week? Why wouldn't she be happy with a rich son-in-law?

"Mom's right you know," Monique says when they are doing the dishes. "You have gone a little overboard since you've been working. She's just worried you're trying to buy happiness and you'll end up disappointed."

Jaqueline stares at her sister through narrowed eyes. "Finish the fucking dishes yourself."

She throws the tea towel at Monique, "I have to go to work."

She slams the screen door as she leaves.

"Ladies don't swear." Monique yells out the door and laughs.

Jaqueline would tell parts of this story to Peter later on, using it to great advantage over fancy drinks in the Gateway Lounge. Through a veil of tears and tinkling ice-cubes she told him how persecuted she was living at home with women who had no ambition, no wish to better themselves, no man to take care of them.

Peter moved his chair closer to her, dabbing her tears with his white hankie and told her she was ruining her make-up and his hankie before putting his arm around her and asking her to be his wife.

This is all according to Jaqueline's plan. His salary potential as a civil servant is beyond her expectations and it is only a bonus that he is handsome.

II

It was the kind of social engagement Jaqueline hated. The night was interminable. They were sitting at a crowded table in the bar of the Royal Hotel. This was their first trip to Peter's childhood home. She was being honoured - Peter introduced her to the guys he grew up with. His sister Ethel was horrified to discover where he was taking her.

"But Peter," said Ethel, "you can't take a pregnant woman to the bar!"

"Why not?"

"Sometimes its best just to stay out of the public eye, while...you know."

"What's the matter Ethel? Afraid people will be reminded of having sex if I take Jaqueline out in public?"

"Well! Peter, Its almost indecent exposure. I didn't even go to church while I was expecting John."

"Ethel, I want to show off my wife to the guys I grew up with. I want them to see what good taste I have."

"And prove his manhood," Jaqueline piped up and patted her enormous belly," The only reason he'll take me out in public these days is to say 'Hey! Look what I did everybody!' "

Jaqueline was watching the other tables in the Ladies and Escorts section of the bar. Couples would wander in, order a beer and chat quietly for a while before leaving. The table next to them changed people three times since they arrived.

She was interested to see what other women were wearing, what colour lipstick or eye make-up they wore. It didn't do to lose touch with fashion these days. Living in the bush the way they did, it was easy to find yourself out of touch with the rest of society. Mind you she thought, we are in a bar, its not like this was a lounge or anything, not like there are a lot of classy women in here. No, Peter had to take me to a bar, couldn't meet his friends at a place where you take a lady because they wouldn't know how to act.

Jaqueline was becoming very angry. She listened to cliche after cliche.

"Hey Stretch, how's the weather up there?"

"Geez you old lady killer didn't think you had it in you to settle down."

"So tell me Mrs. Peter, is he as good in bed as he brags?"

"They tell me tall men have really small equipment, is that true? Does he make you happy? Wanna go out to the alley and have a look at mine? I may be short, but hey, I make women happy!"

She felt an elbow dig into her side. Jaqueline refrained from sneering but she gave Peter the lets go soon signal. It didn't work. She watched them down beer after beer, watched their mouths grinning, full of bad teeth while they told bawdy jokes and had laugh after laugh. Jaqueline sat and smoked cigarette after cigarette and nursed a beer the whole evening. She smiled when it was expected and exchanged appropriate nods and murmurs with the guys.

Peter was ignoring her pleas to end the evening. Jaqueline got up to go to the washroom and suffered yet another bout of jokes about pregnant women and their bladders. When she finished washing her hands she continued out of the bar into the lobby where she called a cab. She doubted she would be missed very quickly.

Ethel looked at her with surprise when she walked in the door by herself.

Jaqueline said nothing to Ethel as she walked past her to the bedroom, closed the door. "He'll pay for this someday," she said outloud and started to cry.

III

The nuns wouldn't let her see her baby. She was standing at the nurses station demanding to see her daughter. A nun stood in front of her barring her way, arms crossed, her black clad body an iron gate Jaqueline was having trouble getting through.

Jaqueline and Peter brought Fiona into emergency ten days ago. She was vomiting and had diarrhea. They waited three hours for the diagnosis.

"Gastroenteritis," said the Doctor. "She'll have to stay for a while...advanced state...watch her round the clock...extremely dehydrated. Why didn't you bring her in earlier?"

Jaqueline and Peter made the 20 mile trip back home and waited for the Doctor to phone and tell them to come and get the baby. Three nights ago he called to say she almost died. Peter was working the graveyard shift. Jaqueline couldn't drive a car. It was a week since she was at the hospital. Peter tried to see the baby but the nuns turned him away. Weak, Jaqueline thought. How could a bunch of old ladies keep a father from his child.

Jaqueline could hear a chorus of children crying, some calling for their mothers. She hated the nuns. What did they know about babies? She looked passed Sister Agatha down the long hospital corridor. Jaqueline considered walking straight past her, searching every room until she found Fiona. Was one of the criers her baby? She wasn't really sure she was missing her, couldn't really remember the sound of her cry or the shape of her face, but well, this was nonsense, Fiona didn't belong to the nuns, she belonged to her.

"But Madam, the child has been through a dangerous ordeal. You can give thanks to the Lord that Dr. Paul was making his rounds when he did, the baby would have been dead by morning." The sister spoke authoritatively with a French accent.

"I want to see my baby now."

She stared the old woman in the eyes. Grey like the hair that was sticking out from the woman's wimple. They all looked the same. Jaqueline had no fear of the nuns. She was not brought up Catholic, the weight of venal and mortal sin did not rest on her shoulders. She did not care to know the difference.

Neither did Jaqueline attend the Catholic school like her friend Mary so she felt the nuns did not have authority over her. She remembered Mary brought to tears one day while they were walking downtown. Both girls were young and beautiful, wearing lipstick in public for the first time, long before either of them were married. The nuns stopped them and berated Mary for painting her lips like a common harlot. Silly old bats Jaqueline thought, I hope this one likes Poppy Red. She pursed her lips.

Another child started wailing at the end of the long corridor. She remembered how mean the nuns had been to her when she came to the hospital to have her baby. They strapped her arms and legs to the delivery table so she couldn't move. They told her to shut up and be quiet when she cried out with her pains. They told her to stop squirming so it would be easier for the doctor. Jaqueline felt the anger burning deep in her chest. She wanted to take the crucifix that dangled down the side of her full skirt and strangle her with it.

"Let me speak to the Doctor. NOW."

The sun shone through the large window reflecting off the yellow walls of the hospital room, bathing all five of the children in this room in an institutional glow. It was quiet in here and calm.

Jaqueline, petite and well dressed, rushed into the room and searched each of the six cribs anxiously looking at each child. Five of them were sleeping, the sixth was standing holding onto the sides of her crib bouncing slightly. With a cry of disappointment she rushed out of the room.

The doctor brought her back.

"Why, Mrs. Loewen here is your daughter." He stood beside the child bouncing in the crib.

"That's not my baby! A mother recognizes her child! She doesn't look anything like the baby I brought in here ten days ago! What have you monsters done to her?"

The baby in the crib stopped bouncing, looked like she was deciding whether or not to cry.

" Look Mrs. Loewen, this is the same little girl you brought to emergency ten days ago, and the same one I delivered for you just under a year ago. I would like to keep her here for another day or two, however since you seem to be so anxious, I'll let you take her home today as long as you bring her to the clinic next Monday."

Jaqueline lifted Fiona out of the crib, walked out of the room, down the long corridor to the sister waiting at the nurses station.

"You bitch," she whispers to the nun as she passes her in the hall. "You've changed babies on me and I can't prove it."

Jaqueline becomes a saint when she tells this story at coffee with the other ladies. She's practised it over the years, retells it to a new audience whenever they move. Her lips coloured in Avon's Salmon Pink lipstick embellish the words as they pass out into the world. She tells about walking down the long green corridor, searching all the rooms not being able to find her baby. She is panicking, thinking they accidentally gave Fiona away to someone else when the Doctor comes running and takes her to a room with six little waifs in white iron cribs.

"I didn't even recognize my own baby! Look at her now. Except for the nose that looks like it came from Peter's family, I'd still not be convinced that I actually gave birth to that child." She points at Fiona colouring pictures with two other little girls.

"They were so incompetent they could have sent babies home with the wrong parents. The smell of shit was overpowering. Those goddamned nuns know nothing of taking care of babies. I'd be surprised if they changed their diapers more than once a day. Took three weeks to get rid of the rash! Did I ever give the Doctor a piece of my mind."

The women all take drags from their cigarettes, blow the smoke up at the ceiling and shake their heads. They all have a story of doctor or nurse incompetence. They compare notes, seeing who has had to endure the worst. Soon they all go home herding their children in front of them leaving Jaqueline to clean up the lipstick remains of morning gossip on cups and cigarette butts.

IV

"Mommy, Mommy!"

Jaqueline gets up from her weeding, turns and sees Fiona running toward her. There is a bunch of dandelions clenched in her little chubby hand. Fiona is running with her hand outstretched.

"Mommy, Mommy flowers for you."

Jaqueline waits for the girl to reach her.

"Pretty flowers, Mommy, like the ones Daddy brought."

Peter was always bringing her flowers. Other women thought this was romantic, she just thought it was to appease his guilt. She always knew when she got flowers he was feeling guilty for some minor or major transgression; drinking too much on the weekend, or looking at another woman. Having an affair was sure to bring two weeks of flowers every night, boxes of chocolates and a steak dinner in a fancy restaurant.

"Thank you Fiona," Jaqueline puts the dandelions on the ground beside her and continues weeding.

"Mommy....they need water."

"Oh for heavens sake. Take them to Auntie Monique in the kitchen and tell her to put them in water and then put them on the window in front of the sink."

God, now I'll have wilted dandelions all summer by the kitchen sink. Roses they aren't. She hums along with the tune from the radio, the sound coming through the open living room window. Monique goes home tomorrow. Two weeks is long enough to recover from the abortion. She should never have got into trouble in the first place. I told her Steve would have no respect for her if she went to bed with him before getting a ring.

"Mommy, Mommy."

"Not again," Jaqueline groans quietly and gets up from her weeding.

"A chocolate bar Mommy, a chocolate bar!"

Fiona is running toward her again with her little hand straight in front of her. There is something that looks like an overgrown cigar in her hand.

"See Mommy, a chocolate bar, like daddy brought you with the flowers."

Jaqueline bends down to take a close look at what the child is holding out to her. A foul smell invades the space between the two faces.

"Fiona Louise! That is dog shit. Poop! Dirty! Put it down right this second. No! Don't wipe your hands on your dress. March right into the bathroom. Don't touch anything! Keep your hands away from the walls."

Jaqueline grabs her hand and drags the howling child to the washroom.

"Stop squirming!"

She shakes the child. Fiona's head hits the corner of the sink vanity. She starts bawling even louder.

"Shut up!" Jaqueline slaps Fiona's face and continues to wash her hands. Finally they are clean.

"Fiona will you stop crying now!."

She stoops to look the girl in the eyes and notices a pool of blood on the floor. Blood soaked the back of Fiona's dress from her shoulder to her waist. The child is crying uncontrollably.

"Monique! Get the car, I have to take Fiona to the Doctor."

"Fiona needed two stitches to close the wound in her head," Monique is telling Peter when he gets home from work. She is sitting at the table trying to coax a silent Fiona to take a treat. The child has not spoken or smiled since the doctor visit. Jaqueline has just finished taking a picture trying to make the little girl smile.

"Daddy," Fiona holds her arms over her shoulder waiting to be lifted high. She smiles finally.

"I'm leaving in the morning," Monique tells her sister as they sip after dinner coffee. "Mom would never approve of how you treat your daughter."

"Hey, that was an accident!"

"Don't be such a prude, if you hadn't over reacted about the doggie log there wouldn't have been a trip to the doctor. Besides if it was an accident why didn't you tell him the truth instead of saying she fell against the coffee table when she was playing."

"You're one to talk," Jaqueline bites back and sneers in her sister's face, a lit cigarette between her fingers. "Mom wouldn't approve of your abortion either. When it comes to child abuse, I guess we're on equal footing. Don't bother to come back for a visit."

*   *   *

On summer evenings when Fiona was little, when the top of her head
came up to his kneecap father took her for a walk. Always after supper, just
before her bath. Outside he would hold one finger of his hand out to her.
Fiona would grab it with her little hand, hold on tight because she didn't
want to lose Daddy. He took long leisurely strides, throwing his left foot
out at an angle, the instep pointing almost forward, the heel at 7 o'clock.
Fiona ran or hippity hopped beside him holding on to that one finger.
When she was tired he lifted her onto his shoulders. She was the tallest
person in the world then. The neighbours would confuse her, come and
ask how the weather was up there, call father Stretch, not Peter. She could
see pink skin on the top of Mr. Beverly's head. Father said this happened a
lot when you're tall; seeing things other people couldn't from down low,
like a bird hiding in a tree or the dust on the top of mother's fridge, or
Fiona over top of the stair railing at night sitting listening to mother and
father when she was supposed to be in bed. Fiona giggled, let me down.
She held on to the outstretched finger, took big giant steps to keep up
with father throwing her left foot out at an angle slightly, the heel at 7
o'clock both of them singing MARY HAD A LITTLE LAMB.

*   *   *

The sun spot on the kitchen floor took all morning to reach the stool
where she sat perched by the kitchen counter. As it edged onto the pages
of her book Jaqueline looked at her watch to see what time it was. Shit she
thought, almost noon, and she was only two thirds of the way through the
book. She didn't want the interruption making lunch would bring. Peter
never came home for lunch and now that school was out she resented the
imposition of her morning routine. She marked her place with her coffee
spoon and went over to the window. If she stood on her tip toes and
looked sideways to her right she could still see the kids standing around
watching the moving van down the street. Quickly she made a peanut butter and jam sandwich, put it on a plate and covered it with Saran Wrap. She
made another cup of instant coffee and sat down to read her book again.
The girl would come in to eat if she was hungry. She lit her cigarette, if she
was lucky Fiona would go for lunch at one of her friends' houses. For now
though she'd have some time to herself.

The book she was reading was something she found on the shelf by
Peter's side of the bed, one of those detective stories where the hero was a
male that drank, smoked and bedded women so much it was amazing he
had time to solve the crime. Jaqueline was looking for Peter's Playboy magazines when she came across this book. It looked a little more interesting

than the latest issue of True Story. It was a man's book, with a lot of sex in it. Ladies books weren't always so much fun. Jaqueline undid her zipper, ran her hand over her belly and down between her legs. The book made her excited. She liked the feel of herself aroused, all warm, soft and wet. She liked the smell of herself on her fingers. She kept reading, turning pages with one hand, closing her eyes imagining that what was happening to the detectives latest heroine was happening to her. Her orgasm came the same time as the woman in the book. She pulled her hand out of her pants, did up her zipper. Smelled her fingers before wiping them on the side of her pants. She sighed. Took a drink of coffee lit another cigarette and kept reading.

All morning the group of children watched the men from the moving company. They stood, sat, chewed gum, yelled insults, threw rocks at each other, threw rocks at the truck. They talked about who might be moving in, watched the boxes and furniture the men carried into the Green's old house. It was the beginning of July. Under the hot sun the men sweated in their dark blue overalls. The children listened to them cursing the heat or the owners of the furniture as they lugged the heavy loads into the house.

The man with the name John embroidered in red on his overalls carried a clip board and called the other men incompetent assholes if they dropped anything or lazy SOB's if he thought they were moving too slow.

"What does incompetent mean?" Shelley leaned over and asked Fiona in a whisper.

Fiona shrugged her shoulders.

Phil leaned over and said in a whisper, "It's when you don't work right...you know...either you have diarrhea or you're constipated."

"Oh," said Shelley and Fiona together.

Fiona was thinking about this when Shelley whispered to her again, "That man with Jack on his uniform?"

"Uh-huh."

"Is he ever fat."

"Shhh!" said Lisa. "He might hear you."

"He's the fattest, baldest man I've ever seen," whispered Shelley.

"Where do you think he buys his overalls?" snickered Phil.

"Not Robinson's Stores," laughed Kenny real loud.

"Maybe Marshall Wells," said Fiona

"No," David told them, "The moving company probably custom makes them."

"They should make him some hair too," Kenny laughed and threw a rock at the orange truck.

Fiona, Lisa, and Shelly giggled.

They all watched Jack grunt and groan carrying one side of a big chest of drawers. Sweat rolled down from the top of his bald head into his red face. He made the man with the name Roy on his overalls stop and put the piece of furniture down on the ground while he wiped his forehead with a hankie he took out of his right hip pocket. Roy stood and whistled Foghorn Leghorn's theme song as he waited. Fiona thought Jack might melt away in the summer heat, the way the fat on the edge of the pork-chops melted when mother cooked them under the broiler.

This was the most exciting thing that happened since school was let out a week ago. They watched closely to see if the men brought anything out of the truck that might indicate there were kids in this unknown fami-ly. The boys looked for bicycles with a bar, or go-carts. The girls looked to see if there were girl's bicycles. Fiona looked carefully to see if there was a canopy bed. This would be a sure sign of a girl. She dreamed of having a canopy bed. Every time the new Eatons or Simpsons catalogues came she would turn to the bed section and check to see if they still had them. A girl who slept in a canopy bed would be someone she would like to be friends with, maybe mother might even let her have one if she had a friend who did.

The man with the name John on his overalls said, "Okay guys trucks empty." He turned around and whistled at the children.

"Hey! You kids! Get across the street," He waved his arm as if it were a fly swatter.   "Back there," he pointed, "so no one gets hurt when the truck backs up."

They all moved obediently to where he pointed. Phil told them about the boy in Winnipeg who was run over by a moving truck last summer while it was backing up. Shelly said he was a cousin of her cousin's next door neighbour. He had been watching from a sidewalk too.

"Hey! Mister!" yelled Kenny, "Know if there's any kids moving in there?"

"How the hell should I know?" the man with the name John yelled back. "Now, outa the way!"

"I guess not," Phil kicked a rock from the side of the road.

"Just a bunch of ugly furniture," Kenny put his hands in his jeans pock-ets.

Silence settled over them as they watched the truck turn the corner at the end of their street and disappear.

"What should we do now?" asked Lisa.

"Who wants to play Mother May I?" Shelly yelled.

"Hey look!" Kenny yelled as he ran across the street into the Green's old yard.

"They left a box," yelled David. "Lets go."

The rest of the gang followed. The men left a packing crate behind. Made of plain coloured wood, its blond sides gleamed in the sunlight. The children ran to where it sat on the green grass. Touched it with their hands running them over the smooth wood, watching for splinters. It was huge, big enough for two kids to fit into it.

Fiona remembered her mother unpacking boxes just like that when they moved here. She remembered mother carefully pulling out the dishes with the red roses and the frosty coloured glasses with the gold leaves on them she was never allowed to drink out of because they were for company.

"We could use it for our fort," called Phil running to the box.

"We could make it into a house," said Shelley as they all arrived at the side of the box.

"We saw it first," said David. "It belongs to us guys."

"Us girls can use it too," said Lisa. "We could take it apart and divide it in half and each use it for our forts."

They all circled the box touching its smooth sides talking about its possibilities.

"Maybe we should save it and use it to keep our things in at the outdoor rink!" said David.

"Yeah!" said Kenny and Lisa at the same time.

"Naa," said Phil, "There is no top, and no way for us to put a lock on it."

"Oh...yeah, I guess that's true," said Kenny a little sadly.

"I know!" said David, "We could play police hide and seek."

"What's that?" asked Fiona.

"Us boys are the police." said David turning the box upside down and claiming the box by sitting on it. "You girls have to do what we say or you have to go in jail." He kicked his foot on the side of the box. The wood made a thunk thunk sound. Fiona felt the backs of her knees tingle.

"Aw, we don't always have to do what you say," said Brenda. "Right Fiona?"

Fiona nodded. She began to have a bad feeling about police hide and seek. She didn't think it would be much fun. As the tingle behind her knees got stronger, Fiona prayed her mother would call her in to do a job, or say they were going shopping today instead of tomorrow.

"Well, I'll count to a hundred while you girls hide. Then we'll look for you, just like hide and seek. When we catch you, you go in jail while we count to 100 again or maybe 500 for longer punishment if you don't cooperate."

"Okay," said Lisa, "then we'll trade places and we can be the police."

"Maybe," said Phil.

"We'll only play if you count to 200 under the box so you can't see where we hide," said Brenda.

"Okay," yelled the boys all at the same time as they scrambled under the box and started counting.

"Hey," said Lisa, "hold on a minute!"

"FIFTEEN!" yelled David.

"You haven't given us any time to decide if we want to play," said Fiona.

"Twenty," yelled Phil. "And if you don't want to play we'll put you in here anyway."

Fear sent Fiona running. She knew exactly where she was going. She'd hidden there before when she was afraid mother would be mad at her for breaking one of her new ashtrays. She ran straight to the Anderson's raspberry patch and crawled to the very back by the fence. It took three hours for father to find her before and maybe they would be finished that horrible game before she had to come out. She thought of how dark it would be under the box. She thought of how long it takes for anyone to count to 100 or even 500 and the tingly feeling started coming back behind her knees. She began to cry and laid down on her tummy in the dirt. She was careful to tuck her feet behind the bushes. Fiona tried not to feel the sting of the scratches on her legs from crawling through the raspberries. Mosquitoes swarmed her. She could hear Lisa screaming and laughing as the boys carried her off to jail. Fiona's eyes filled with tears and she began to cry silently. She was so afraid. She couldn't move now or they would find her. Kenny's feet had already gone by and so had Phil's. Fiona listened to her breathing and thought maybe it was too loud. She tried to hold her breath, but couldn't for long. She practised breathing slowly because that was quieter.

She watched a caterpillar crawl across the dirt in front of her. It was a fuzzy black and yellow one. When it got as far as the fence she raised her head to see if she could see anyone. Nothing. All Fiona could hear was the lazy buzzing of summer bugs and the wind rustling in the Anderson's garden.

This was comforting. This was safe. Anything was better than playing that stupid game, even risking what mother would say about the tear in her new shorts.

Fiona stayed perfectly still. She listened as they caught Lisa and Shelley. She heard them asking where Fiona was. The boys even sent Shelley to see if she was in the house.

"Its time for a posse," said Phil. "Lisa and Shelley are on our side searching for the fugitive. Spread out everyone." All the kids were calling for her. She really couldn't move now. They were all looking for her, even Lisa and Shelley and Brenda. They wouldn't protect her anymore. They'd think she'd have to have her turn in jail now, just like them.

"F-I-O-N-A!!!!!"

"FEEEE-OOOOOOOW-NNAAAAA."

"WHERE ARE YOU?"

"COME OUT, COME OUT, WHEREVER YOU ARE."

Fiona waited until their voices moved on, they sounded like they were at the Thompson's three doors past the Andersons' and four doors from the Green's old house.

Fiona lay and waited. Every time she thought of getting up to run home free she got that tingly feeling behind her legs. She listened as her friends walked farther away calling her name constantly. Then she heard them coming back. Fiona was wondering if she could last until everyone was called in for supper.

"Lets play something else now," said Shelley. "Fiona has a really good hiding place and we'll never find her."

"I know!" David exclaimed, "Lets walk around yelling to her that we are playing something else, then she'll come out of her hiding spot and we'll grab her."

"That's not really fair," said Lisa. "But it could be fun."

"What if she gets home free?" asked Kenny.

"Well, then she's safe, that's the rule, but if we fool her, she won't even try," said David.

"Okay, lets try it," said Phil.

"F-I-O-N-A!!!!"

"FEEEE-OOOOOW-NNAAAAA."

"WHERE ARE YOU???"

"COME OUT, COME OUT, WHEREVER YOU ARE!!"

"WE'RE PLAYING SOMETHING ELSE NOW!"

Fiona listened as they passed and waited for their voices to sound far away. She crawled out of the raspberries slowly and quietly. She could see the kids moving down the street still calling her name. Fiona crawled til she got to the end of the Anderson's drive way, then stood up.

She looked up and down the street considering her options. She could run back to the box and claim home free, or she could run home and stay in her room for the rest of the day. She gauged how much time she'd have to reach home free. She could just make it, it would take longer to run home.

Suddenly she felt the neck of her shirt pulled from the back and something cool slide down her back.

"It's a frog, i's a frog," Kenny yelled.

Startled, Fiona began to scream running all the way back to the Green's old house, grabbing the back of her shirt and pulling it away from her body hoping that what ever was in there would fall out. When she reached the Green's yard she turned on Kenny and chased him around the white house. Round and round they ran, terror and anger burning inside her chest. She forget about the jail. With one burst of speed she caught Kenny the third time round and punched him in the arm.

He laughed, "It didn't hurt."

Fiona punched him again. Kenny stuck his tongue out at her.

"It was only grass anyway," he lunged toward her and grabbed her arm. "You're under arrest," he sneered at her.

"NO," She screamed. "NO....I AM NOT GOING IN THERE."

The other kids had caught up to them by this time and were watching the chase until Kenny caught her. Then they joined in the arrest. Phil picked up Fiona's kicking feet, David lifted up the box.

"Its not so bad Fiona," Lisa said. "Its kinda like a little house."

"NO!....NO!...NO!" Fiona screamed in terror, tears running down her face. She squirmed to try and get free from Phil and Kenny. "I'm afraid! Its too small! I can't go under here!"

Shelley started chanting, "Fraidy Cat, Fraidy Cat."

David said, "We'll all count to five hundred and then we'll let you go. It won't take long, you'll see.

The box dropped over Fiona and the sound of bugs and birds and wind disappeared, replaced by a ringing in her ears. The sunshine was blocked out. It was gray under the box, gray like nothing, like when you close your eyes. The tingling behind her knees spread to the rest of her legs, her arms, her chest. Fiona felt like she couldn't breathe. She tried taking big gulps of air. It wasn't enough. She tried to lift the box, six inches of sunshine showed through the bottom.

'Sit on it," said Kenny, "Everybody sit on it, she's trying to escape."

Fiona kept screaming, "LET ME OUT."

"We're only at 50," said Brenda.

"Hold on Fiona," Shelley yelled. "You're turn's almost over."

"NOOOO!" screamed Fiona, "LET ME OUT NOW! NOW! NOW!

She began to kick the box. The boys stared to laugh. Fiona was screaming in terror.

"I CAN'T BREATH, I NEED MORE AIR."

The boys kept laughing.

"Maybe we should let her out," said Lisa. "She doesn't sound too good."

" Maybe we should count to 100. Real slow," said David. "She's being such a sucky baby."

"NOOOOOOOO!" screamed Fiona, her voice becoming hoarse. "NOOOOOO!"

With each no she kicked the side of the box again, and again, harder and harder as her friends laughed and made jokes.

"NO!" she screamed and kicked and kicked until there was a crack where her feet landed. She kept kicking until there was a hole that fresh air came through. She kicked again and again and screamed until the side of the box broke.

Kenny reached 128 when she crawled out, pushed Phil out of the way screaming "NO....NO....NO....NO running off in the direction of home.

*   *   *

It was December 15th. Fiona walked behind father pulling the tobaggan singing JINGLE BELLS, jumping in the big footprints he left in the snow, the pattern of his tracks too long for her stride. This was the day mother decorated the Christmas tree. Father stayed home from work. He sharpened his axe, showed her how to feel its blade using the ridges of her fingerprints. She tried to split one of her hairs on the blade like Elmer Fudd or Wylie E. Coyote did on Bugs Bunny. "Are you sure its sharp enough?" she asked.

Fiona dressed up warm with two pairs of underwear, two pairs of socks, and a toque. Father wore no hat, long underwear and only put his gloves in his pockets. This was their ritual.

Father told her he had picked out two good trees in the summer on his walks through the woods to work. He always cut two to give mother a choice. "Which one do you like best?" mother asked when they got home. They always pointed to the one they liked the least. She always picked that one for the house.

Fiona gave another jump into father's footsteps, singing JINGLE BELLS all over again from the beginning. This was always a good day. She loved the sound of their boots trudging through snow, the smell of father's cigarette smoke in the dry minus 30 weather, the smell that trees made when they were cut down and the smile on mother's face when they came home for hot chocolate with the two most perfect trees the forest had to offer.

*   *   *

"Greyhound buses are the only thing holding our country together," the old guy in the seat in front of Fiona was telling his seat mate. It was the perfect opening line for a rant against politicians. She tuned them out. The bus was just leaving Hope.

Hope. Sounded like a name Saskatchewan should have, probably did. It didn't matter that she was travelling at night. She had seen this road so many times she could tell the landmarks even if it was night. Hope. There was a girl in school called Hope. Hope, Faith, and Charity. The Hope and Faith were girls she new, but the only Charity she ever came across was a tv character on a show like Petticoat Junction. Must be some southern American thing.

Hope for this hope for that...hoping hopping..Here comes Peter Cotton Tail. Easter. Hippity Hop. Easter break. Broken heart. Mother said she knew a man who died of a broken heart. Only love can break your heart, try to be sure right from the start...

*   *   *

"What the hell do you think you were doing?" Robert, white faced, hands clenched at his side. He backed her against the kitchen counter. It was only afterwards she realized how rumpled his clothes were.

"I only did what you once said you would do to me."

"I only said I thought about it." Robert grabbed her shoulders and shook her.

"So did I, thought about it and decided to teach you a lesson." She wasn't afraid of him anymore.

"Teach me a lesson? Teach me a lesson?" He raised his arm, fist still clenched and punched her shoulder.

Fiona laughed.

He punched her again.

"I'm not afraid of you anymore."

Robert punched her shoulder a third time. Tears were running down his cheeks, his face twisted with emotion. Fiona thought he looked like a gargoyle she once saw on Notre Dame Cathedral in Paris.

"Get out of here." He screamed at her over and over.

"I'm already packed"

*   *   *

Fiona took up her position of sentinel on the top stair. After mother and father said their good nights and a suitable amount of time passed she tip toed to the top stair and sit listening to her parents pass the evening until she was either tired enough to fall asleep, or, if it was a bad night she would slip quietly back to her bed, curl up in the blankets with her head under the pillow the way she did with thunderstorms in the summer, or the howling wind in the winter.

Tonight the sound of mother shuffling cards for solitaire, the rustle of father's newspaper, and the tinkle of ice in their drinks was comforting. She liked going downstairs in the morning and finding their empty glasses on the coffee table, along with the abandoned remnants of their evening's activity. Mother's deck of cards sitting neatly and primly on the cleared space on the coffee table. Father's newspaper folded neatly on his chair seat, or the abandoned scrabble game left exactly how they finished it full of words and the score sheet sitting by father's side of the Scrabble board.

This was going to be a good night. She was never sure until she sat on the stairs for a while, what would come. Sometimes the bad nights came in clusters, several nights in a row.

Sometimes they were just once in a while. The morning after the bad nights Fiona found broken dishes, the phone torn out of the wall, mother wearing sunglasses while she got breakfast together. Fiona never asked questions, understood by her parents postures that she wasn't welcome to, that they'd tell her a lie because it wasn't her business.

Tonight she listened to the murmur of conversation. Tried not to pick out words. The mumble was comforting. Periodically they laughed together. Fiona wondered if it was a joke father told or if he was tickling mother. She heard them move to the kitchen, heard cupboard doors banging, then the sound of cooking. A midnight snack, a really good night Fiona smiled.

Fiona tried to guess what she was cooking by the aroma. These were exotic dishes she never tasted. They were special things mother kept only for father and herself. Only made them late at night. Creamed mushrooms on toast was Fiona's favorite. She imagined it must be the food of rich people. It sounded so exotic...creamed mushrooms on toast. She used to hope that she would find it on the menu of restaurants when father took them out for dinner or lunch, but it never showed up....not even at the Gateway Hotel or the La Verandre where father took important guests for steak dinner when they came to town. Sometimes when she knew mother was making this exotic dish she contemplated heading downstairs, saying she couldn't sleep and that she was hungry too, but she didn't want to intrude on any good nights. Once she almost asked mother for creamed mushrooms on toast for lunch, but stoped herself just in time. Mother would have found out her secret, how she watched over them in the evenings.

Tonight it was fried egg sandwiches. Toasted fried egg sandwiches, Fiona heard the toaster pop, the sizzle of eggs in the pan and finally smelled the aroma of everything as it floated up the stairs.

Fiona wandered back to her bedroom, walking on tiptoes, stepping over the creaky spot just before her bedroom door. Maybe tomorrow morning she would find mother's underwear on the floor by the couch like she did once, and mother would pretend it was never there, pick it up quickly in the morning and hide it in the laundry basket.

*   *   *

Jaqueline looked at the clock. Eight pm. Fiona would be on her way by now.

"If Robert doesn't pick me up at the bus station, that means he doesn't want anything to do with me...can I stay with you for a while?" Fiona phoned her a couple of hours ago.

"Where are you?"

"Vancouver."

"That's a long way from Saskatoon."

"We had a bad fight."

"And you left? Jesus Fiona can't you do anything right?"

"Mother, please...."

"Why don't you just stay there with that friend of yours until you find your own place and I'll come out and stay with you. I loved it when you lived there. What the hell did you take the bus for, haven't you ever heard of planes?"

"Mother there's Robert to consider."

"Why? I never liked him anyway. Too serious for words. You always did pick strange boyfriends."

Jaqueline almost said no. What do I need this for she asked herself. She'll arrive with her funny clothes and her funny hair and her funny ideas about life. She is not graceful, my daughter...she'll clump around here, make dinners I don't want to eat and think she's helping me out. How did she ever come from me? She changed the channel on the television, laid out another game of solitaire. Ace up, red two on black three, black eight on red nine. She felt lonely often, but she had the tv. Daytime was alright, there were people she could call, or go for coffee with. But the nights were interminable. So much of her life she lived for the dark, the evening hours. Motherhood was a job, quitting time was as soon as dinner was made, she was through for the day. The nights were her own and she selfishly guarded them. Now she just got through the nights until it was daylight and her life began again. The nights, oh they were long. The empty bed, the cold nights, the need for pajamas. Jaqueline shuffled her cards, laid out another game of solitaire. Looking for another show to lose herself in, watching tv until she couldn't keep her eyes open then fall asleep wherever she pleased until the morning.

*　　*　　*

Jaqueline stared at the mess in the bathtub. She had just cleaned it this morning, now half inch hairs clung to the sides and bottom of the tub. She flushed the toilet, washed her hands and yelled.

"Fiona Louise git in here right now."

The girl came on the run. She always did. Thirteen years old and Jaqueline could count on her appearing before she finished yelling her name at moments like this.

"What the hell is this mess all about?"

"I shaved my legs."

Jaqueline stared at the pimple on Fiona's cheek. It had fascinated her since it appeared yesterday. She would watch it move whenever Fiona talked or ate. She wondered why Fiona hadn't squeezed it.

"I told you on Monday you don't need to shave yet. If you take the peach fuzz off, the hair will just grow back black and wiry and you'll have to do it for the rest of your life."

"It wasn't peach fuzz anymore and the girls always make fun of me because I wear leotards and not panty hose."

"For Christ's sake! You're supposed to listen to your mother who knows something not a bunch of 13 year old girls who don't. I guess if they told you to jump off a cliff you would?"

"They were already black and they looked like spider legs."

Jaqueline raised her eyebrow. The girl actually yelled at her. She even looked angry.

"Spider legs? Spider legs! Good God Fiona, how could you be so stupid? I've heard some good ones...wait til I tell your father. Get this cleaned up in the next five minutes or else. Supper will be ready when your finished."

Jaqueline took a sip of her after dinner coffee. Little Miss Muffet was cleaning the kitchen. She called her that when she told her to do the dishes. Little Miss Muffet she chuckled and recited under her breath. Little Miss Muffet sat on a tuffet eating her curds and whey. Along came a spider and sat down beside her and frightened Miss Muffet away.

"What did you say?" Peter lowered a corner of his newspaper and looked at her.

"Along came a spider."

"Oh." He looked at her for a moment then went back to reading his paper.

Along came a spider and sat down beside her. Poor little Miss Muffet. A spider beside her. The picture in Fiona's old nursery rhyme book had a little girl in petticoats sitting on a stool under a tree with a spider dangling from a branch at eye level, then a picture of an overturned stool and the little girl running away.

"Spider legs, really!" she exclaimed out loud, remembering how Fiona, three years old, got the nickname Little Miss Muffet.

The girl was screaming in the basement. Jaqueline jumped from the couch, dropping her True Story magazine on the coffee table. She could tell it was sheer fright. It was the way she imagined someone would scream if they found a mutilated body. Jaqueline rushed down the stairs. The child was terrified. Her face was red and blotched. There were tears running down her face. Two inches from her left foot was a Daddy Long Legs spider.

"Mom," the girl said and pointed her finger at it.

"Jesus Christ Fiona! It's just a goddamned spider! Do you know what you do with spiders?"

Jaqueline stepped on it and turned her foot squishing the spider until it was a wet stain on the concrete.

"There, that's what you do to spiders." She turned her back on the whimpering child and stomped up the stairs wiping her foot on the rug at the top to make sure no spider juice was tracked onto the clean kitchen floor.

Jaqueline shook her head and made her way back to the couch and the magazine. She told the child to play with her toys until supper time. Periodically she could hear her hiccupping and an occasional outburst of crying. It was just a stupid spider she thought. Jaqueline finished her latest issue of True Story and picked up the current issue of The Star Weekly.

Jaqueline lit a DuMaurier, took a long drag and exhaled. Ten years later and the girl was still afraid of spiders. She took a sip of her after dinner coffee and another hit from her cigarette. She cringed listening to Fiona singing as she did the dishes.

The girl was almost finished. It had taken years but slowly Jaqueline had trained her to clean the kitchen immaculately. She reached for a deck of cards on the coffee table and began shuffling them. She knew when she went to refill her coffee cup the kitchen would sparkle and all would be perfect, except for the ashtrays. Lately Fiona had begun to pile ashtrays by the sink refusing to wash them. There were four or five of them there already. At least two days accumulation

Peter finished the paper and was playing his favourite records. The television had been broken for a week and Jaqueline was tired of listening to their record collection. He danced over to her wiggling his hips in her face, a glass of rye in his right hand, a cigarette in his left.

"Come dance with me."

"Peter this isn't the June ball."

" Along came a spider and sat down beside her." He winked at her and danced away to change the record.

Jaqueline lit another cigarette and shuffled the cards a little more. She moved the days accumulation of papers and letters to one end of the table. Oh God not again. I hope old man Profit fixes that tv soon. Can't take much more of this night after night. The Mormon Tabernacle choir had just begun the Hallelujah Chorus for the third time. Peter and Fiona joined in. Jaqueline's nerves were wearing thin. The least they could do is both sing in unison. Jaqueline put the cigarette in her mouth and puffed continuously while she laid out a game of solitaire.

It was a fast game. The deck won too quickly. She put the cards down and butted her cigarette. Fiona's report card sat on the top of the pile of papers. She picked it up and looked at it again. 'Fiona is a conscientious student.' The report card read. Almost every teacher had written a complementary comment. 'Good performance', and 'Fiona is an eager student.' Nothing a parent could complain about.

"Very nice Fiona, " she told her this afternoon. "If only you could be just as conscientious and eager at cleaning your room or washing your face."

Jaqueline pointed to the pimple on Fiona's cheek. She watched the girl's eyes fill with tears. With a small feeling of satisfaction she turned her attention back to cooking dinner.

The girl, the baby, her, the child. Jaqueline rarely called her by name.

"You have to name her sooner or later," her mother said after the baby was born.

Name it! She couldn't even look at it. Jaqueline couldn't figure out exactly how she could have let herself get in this predicament. And Peter was so proud! He was a real man now. She couldn't quite understand, other than that, exactly why she needed to be a mother.

The baby was so ugly. She had such a pretty little outfit to bring it home in. She would have thought a handsome man like him would make a pretty baby. The nurses and her mother said the baby would look different in three months. They said it was just the birth that distorted the features. But the little thing was so dependent. Jaqueline had no admiration for people who where dependent on others. After a day she gave up trying to match pretty names to an ugly baby. She let Peter pick the name.

"Fiona bring me another cup of coffee."

Jaqueline watched her daughter walk into the room to get her cup. Peter was playing Paul Anka. He waltzed over to her and sat beside her on the couch. His arm draped over her shoulders. He is a handsome man she thought proudly. He gave her shoulder a squeeze and placed a wet kiss on her cheek.

"I'm just a lonely boy, lonely and blue, I'm all alone, with nothing to do."

Peter fancied himself a singer. He reeked of rye.

"Guess what I want to do later? Sit on your tuffet," he whispered in her ear."

"Peter."

"Hey honey," he called to Fiona as the girl brought the requested cup of coffee, "Give your old man a kiss. I live with the two most beautiful women in town."

"Peter you're drunk."

"Jesus a man can't have an after dinner drink around here without you saying something." He left the couch and went to flip the record over.

"Fiona go finish the kitchen and stop gawking"

She took a sip of her coffee. The second side of Paul Anka's greatest hits played on the stereo. She thought of the pimple on Fiona's cheek. That pimple was ugly. It made Fiona look ugly. Lately people were telling Jaqueline how pretty the child was becoming. She looked for the signs herself but just couldn't see what other people saw. Last week Jaqueline had taken Fiona shopping for her first bra. She had overheard Mrs. Burns tell Sheila in the Grand Clothing Company about how much prettier Fiona was then her mother at the same age.

"I'm afraid," she told the women after she had overheard the comment, "that I can't find anything that will suit. It appears the quality is not what I would have expected for the price you're charging."

Jaqueline smiled as she left the store leaving Mrs. Burns and Sheila standing at the counter boxes of training bras in a mountain by the cash.

"Mom I thought those bras looked alright. I liked the lacy one."

"It's your first bra, what do you know about anything. Robinsons Stores will have anything you might need. Besides I really think young girls your age should still be wearing undershirts."

"But Mom..."

"Shut up Fiona. You may have already had you're first period but it doesn't mean you should wear a bra."

Prettier indeed! Her legs will never be as nice as mine. She does too much running. Mine will always be slimmer. There is too much of Peter's family in her.

"Oh, please, stay by me....Diana"

Jaqueline lit another cigarette. I wish the baby sitters had worn that record out.

Actually, Jaqueline thought, Fiona was turning out the wrong way. She had tried to teach her to be a lady, with all the proper manners. She had some success. She didn't have to be ashamed about how her daughter behaved in public. The things Jaqueline was disappointed in were her dubious taste in clothes, she never wore a dress; the way she wanted to wear her hair, long and parted in the middle; the hours the girl spent reading in her room; and there was her interest in sports, all that running and perspiring. Really, she wasn't very lady like. God knows she had done her best, there just wasn't the affinity between them one would have expected.

"Oh I love you gal and I need you Peggy Sue..."

God he was playing Buddy Holly now.

At supper Peter had praised the girl for another good report card. Jaqueline watched the pimple move up and down while Fiona ate.

"Do many kids at school get detentions?" she blurted.

"Yeah," Fiona looked surprised. "Lots of kids."

"Have you ever been in trouble at school?"

Fiona shook her head. "No." Her brown eyes looked back at Jaqueline. "How come?"

"Jaqueline!" Peter exclaimed.

"I don't want to get the strap," the girl replied, her eyes were frightened.

Coward. Jaqueline thought. She's afraid of her own shadow. No backbone. You could control the girl with anger. She often wondered when she would rebel. Jaqueline pushed and pushed the limits but the girl never wavered, always compliant, always afraid to be punished.

The girl had finished the kitchen and was heading to her room.

"Fiona, its time to steam your face. It would probably help get rid of that thing on your cheek. Set it up in the dinning room."

She watched her daughter assemble the facial sauna she had borrowed from Beth. The bottom reminded Jaqueline of a baby bottle warmer.

"Did you fill the bottom with water?"

"Yes"

"Now wait for it to boil, then you put the funnel shaped part on the top, then steam your face in the opening for 15 minutes."

"Okay."

"Then go and splash cold water on your face. When you're finished put it away carefully, we only borrowed it you know."

"I know."

Jaqueline wondered if Fiona ever thought about putting her finger in the water. She wondered if she would turn blue like the murder victim in that Perry Mason book she read. She stared hard at the girl, imagining life without her. They'd have to get Reverend Carpenter at the United Church to do the funeral because Peter had turned away from his Mennonite roots. They would have to bury her in that yellow lace dress the girl hardly ever wore. Fiona said she hated it, but it was the only thing that would be appropriate. I could wear that black dress I wore to mother's funeral. Maybe I could get away with that navy suit. Beth would never ask for the facial sauna back. The neighbours would all bring flowers and food. I wouldn't have to cook for a week. Mrs. Burns would be there too saying what a pity she was such a pretty girl, and so respectful. Peter would say they should start again and have another baby, or adopt.

"Good God." she whispered under her breath. "I forgot about that." She butted her cigarette, noticed the ashtray was almost full.

Fiona had gone to her room. Peter was looking through the records again. He had poured himself another drink. She eyed it disapprovingly. And he thinks he's getting something special tonight! Boston Pops next I'll bet she thought, and drank the dregs left in her coffee cup. Jaqueline got up and went to the kitchen to fill her cup again. The kitchen was shining and clean except for the pile of ashtrays. How many more days she wondered before the damn tv would be fixed as Mitch Miller and the Gang began singing.

She hated Mitch Miller. She hated Paul Anka and Buddy Holly. They only had them because of the baby sitters when Fiona was young. The foolish child liked the Cowsills and the Osmond Brothers. Tonight Jaqueline even hated Frank Sinatra and Dean Martin.

Fiona was in her room reading again with that ugly zit on her face while this pile of ashtrays sat here stinking.

"Fiona Louise come here right now."

"I've got sixpence, jolly jolly sixpence..."

"What the hell is this pile of dirty ashtrays all about?"

"I don't smoke, I shouldn't have to wash them. They make my hands stink all day."

"I don't care. They are part of the dishes, understand? Who do you think you are anyway? Make my hands stink, really Fiona, do you think you're better than anyone else?"

"No..."

"Why can't you do anything wrong? Do you have to be a little goodie-goodie all your life? Can't you ever bomb a test at school? Can't you walk on the wrong side of the street sometime? Most kids are bad every now and then, do you ever throw rocks at windows? NO. Do you ever step out of line at school? NO. Can't you squeeze that pimple and risk it getting infected? Do you have to do everything anybody ever tells you? Do you have to be so goddamned good all the time?"

Fiona's face was turning red, there were tears in her eyes. She was gulping great gasps of air trying not to cry.

"And that pimple looks so ugly on your face. My complexion has always been perfect, hardly ever a pimple, even when it's that time of the month. A lady always has a peaches and cream complexion. That pimple is all the bad in you coming out. Why don't you do something about it? Soon you'll have those pussy things all over your face. It's a sign of what is deep down in your soul. I don't know how people can say your getting pretty when things like that can grow on your cheek!"

It took a little longer than usual for the tears to come. They spilled over and ran down the girl's cheeks. Fiona looked as frightened and red and ugly as the day she was born. She ran from the room.

"Don't forget to wash those ashtrays tomorrow, or else," Jaqueline yelled.

Jaqueline walked back into the living room. Peter was snoring on the couch. She turned Mitch Miller off and poured herself a drink. She retrieved Fiona's report card and her Readers Digest from the coffee table and sat in the arm chair beside the missing tv. She could hear Fiona crying in her room. Great gulping sobs the girl was trying to muffle in her pillow. Jaqueline took a small sip of rye. Finally, some quiet. She took the report card in her hand and dribbled enough of her drink onto the white card until it made a stain. Lets see how she explains that one to the teachers, so much for perfection. Jaqueline opened her magazine to where she marked her place with a bent page corner, and found the paragraph were she had left off this afternoon.

*   *   *

Mother is furious. It is the night of the music festival recital. Fiona must be at the school auditorium in 20 minutes. Fiona and her school partners have won the square dance competition, and the trophy for the highest marks in this years festival. Mother has gone to a lot of trouble for the occasion taking Fiona to the hairdresser to have her hair done in the same style as her own.

"We'll all have dinner at the La Verendre the night of the recital mother said when Fiona told her about the trophy.

Fiona was eating a peanut butter sandwich waiting for father to come home from the bar. She was sitting at the kitchen table, a tea towel tucked around her waist so no crumbs could fall on the skirt mother had Mrs Baker make out of the same material as the other three girls.

"You asshole, you're ruining the whole night," mother yelled at father on the phone. She found him at the Gateway Hotel.

"I didn't go to all the trouble of a hairdresser for her to sit here all night." Mother slammed the phone as she hung it up, put her hands over her face and cried. "What are the other mothers going to say?"

Fiona kept her eyes on the gray and white arborite table and looked for the clown shape she always saw when she sat at her place in the kitchen. A long time ago she tried to point it out to mother. She said Fiona was wasting her time, all she could see was a bunch of splotches.

"He said he would come right away." Mother went into the living room to cry on the couch.

Fiona tucked the crusts of her sandwich under the rim of the plate close to her body. Mother wouldn't find them until she was in the car on the way to town. One day she asked if mother would put peanut butter all the way to the edge of the bread so the crusts wouldn't be so dry. She thought mother would understand that this was why she always left her crusts. She thought she might ask again soon.

"Lets go princess," father said, rubbing his hands together. He is big. Takes up all the space in the doorway. The air in the house smells like the air that comes out of the door at the beer parlour when people go in and out.

"You're drunk. You can't drive."

Father calls mother a bitch and tells her to shut up and stay home because she looks like hell. She certainly isn't ready to go out anywhere, and she can't drive a car without a license.

Fiona gets to sit in the front seat for once. She watches as they meet a car. Father lifts two fingers off the steering wheel.

wet kiss on the cheek and pats her shoulder. "I'm proud of you."

When the house lights go up after they are finished the program, Fiona cannot find father. She waits outside by the entrance door for an hour before she walks over to the Gateway Hotel. Joyce at the front desk goes into the bar to see if father is there. Fiona takes a big breath when the door opens...sure enough there's that smell.

In ten minutes they are on the highway home, the drive is slow this time.

"No need to rush Princess, the old lady's mad as a hornet."

Father puts a bottle of beer in an old black sock and drinks it as he drives home. They do not speak of the recital instead they sing Hit the Road Jack.

*   *   *

The light in the bus stop in Kamloops was too bright. Fiona thought if Greyhound wanted to keep its customers they should change to some kind of incandescent lighting, something that hid the dirt and grime a little better. Fluorescent lighting at 10:00 pm highlighted the unwashed walls the dust and foot tracks on the floor, the overflowing garbage bins, the washroom littered with paper towels, water droplets, and the air stale and heavy with the perfume from a couple of hundred women. In the cafeteria display cases the lettuce in the sandwiches drooped in the same style as the hair and purple lines under the eyes of the woman at the cash register. Quitting time was coming and they all needed a shower.

This was supposed to be a supper break, half an hour to stretch your legs. Fiona followed the rest of the passengers, took too long looking for something in the display case and settled for a bag of chips and a coffee. She left the bus station and walked around the parking lot for a few minutes. She could see an A&W not too far away and wondered if she could make it there and back before the bus left. Not likely. She walked back across the pavement to the bus, checked the number before climbing aboard and finding her seat.

I wonder what's happening in the outside world? That's how she thought about this trip, the bus was some kind of capsule, or dome. A world of its own, a metal cylinder hurtling down the highway, over mountains. Fiona and all the other passengers were just travelling companions who put their lives on hold for the time it took to get to their destination point. Earthquakes could happen, bombs could fall, war could break out and Fiona wouldn't know. This was a break in daily life. No telephones, no radio, no news. She could buy a newspaper if she wanted too, but this was against the rules, against the reason she took the bus in the first place. There were two songs lingering in the back of her mind, one

"Why do you do that Daddy?"

"I'm waving."

"Waving? But you only lifted two fingers."

"That's a wave."

"But who could see that?"

"Drivers can tell."

"Oh."

The car is travelling very fast. Fiona can't count the seconds between white lines on the highway. They make the twenty mile trip in ten minutes, just in time for the beginning of the recital. Fiona's part is the last item on the program. Father says he's going to sit in the audience and watch.

"When this is all over, I'll meet you by the entrance." Father gives her a started...*Make the world go away, and take it off my shoulders* or something like that and the other was something about..*stop the world I want to get off.* That's what this bus trip was about. Neutral space in the movement of time. No message machine, no mail, no Robert, no housework, no mother. I'll lose a day and discombubalate myself for the rest of the week, but recovery time will be quick. A plane could do the same thing, except it wasn't long enough. If things get really bad I'll have to take a trip across Canada, drop out for a week, maybe two if I take a round trip.

The rest of the passengers filed onto the bus in spurts. The bus driver climbed into his seat and steered the bus back onto the highway. Night time in Kamloops didn't look exciting from the highway, but any place the aunts used to hang out was probably not too wild. Fiona smiled thinking of the aunts. She was fond of her aunts. Felt they were kindred spirits in a way because of the experiences they went through together. Hardship always did that to people. Made them closer than they would have been otherwise. Aunt Ethel was her favorite traveling companion. Fiona would pick Aunt Ethel to travel with across the country. She was like a security blanket, all efficient and mothering.

Fiona turned off the reading light, she wasn't reading anyway, why pretend. She could see a few people up front had their lights on. Darkness interrupted periodically with discreet little notices of someone's personal space.

The moving bus had a rhythm, was it the hum of the engine, or the wheels on the pavement. It wasn't the kind of rhythm that the train wheels had where you could pick out a sentence, but a constant hum and drone. Fiona put her head back and closed her eyes. Maybe she could sleep. She felt her body go numb, suspended in that moment before deep sleep; where she was aware of everything around her, the people, conversations, a heightened awareness and dreaming at the same time.

*   *   *

Aunt Ethel fumbled in her large black handbag. Fiona glanced sideways at the movement, then quickly turned her head straight again. She did not want Aunt Ethel to know she had witnessed tears. It's a three kleenex afternoon, thought Fiona.

This was the first funeral she had ever attended. If the family had been able to reach mother and father, camping somewhere in the Rockies, maybe she wouldn't have to attend this one. But Aunt Ethel thought at age twelve it would help complete her education about life. "Besides," she said, "if you've already watched Hilda die, her funeral certainly isn't going to hurt."

Fiona looked around the hall. She remembered the aunts' horrified discussion about having to use the Elks Hall for the funeral since the church burned down. The hall was the place for celebrations; weddings and anniversaries, people drank wine and other spirits on the premises. Men and women of dubious character were punished for their mistakes by the circuit court judge when it doubled as the court room every second Tuesday. It was here men belonging to the lodge did secret things they never told anyone about. Hilda had not been married, could they bury her from such a place?

Fiona thought it was just fine. There were new things to look at. She didn't have to stare at the same crack in the plaster that ran down the front wall behind the cross. The purple curtains on the windows in the Elks Hall were a nice change from the banners proclaiming peace and love that burned with the church. The floor here had the same tiles as the church and the same shabby mahogany wainscotting graced the walls. There were curling and baseball trophies and pictures on the wall with men wearing strange purple hats. It looked like the Elks Hall could be a lot of fun.

The Queen and Prince Philip looked down from the wall upon everything with serious expressions on their faces. Fiona sang God Save the Queen inside her head when the choir led everyone in another hymn she didn't know.

Fiona noticed most of her aunts' were crying. Her cousin John said that's what happened at funerals. People did nothing but cry. Even the men. She found this interesting and noticed her uncles coughing and clearing their throats a lot. She looked around to see if any of them had hankies in their hands or tears on their cheeks. Aunt Ethel grabbed the top of her head and turned it to the front. Fiona felt her face turn red.

Right at the front of the hall was a large purple sign with gold lettering. ELKS MOTTO it read:

TO MAKE LIFE SWEETER

MEN BETTER
THE WORLD HAPPIER

The top of the minister's head reached just below the sign. Her cousin Deborah said that this minister was the handsomest she had ever seen, and if she had to go to church, at least looking at him made it easier. Deborah was 16. Fiona didn't think he was as good looking as Uncle Bill or Kelly's brother who worked at the grocery store back home. Mother always said Deborah had bad judgement.

The minister was saying another prayer. "Praise the Lord for all good things." As his booming voice filled the hall, Fiona watched a fly settle on the top of his head. It had been flitting around the flowers surrounding the coffin for a while. Must need a rest, Fiona thought.

Uncle Hank walked to the front to read one of Aunt Hilda's favourite verses. The movement sent the fly zooming in front of Uncle Hank and back to the minister and back in front of Uncle Hank again. He brought his hand up and caught it, squished it and wiped his hand on the side of his pants. Never once did he stopped reading. Fiona wrinkled her nose.

"TCH," said Aunt Ethel.

Fiona stared hard at the ELKS MOTTO again so she didn't laugh. TOMAKELIFESWEETERMENBETTERTHEWORLDHAPPIERTOMAKE-LIFESWEETERMENBETTERTHEWORLDHAPPIER. She read it fast ten times before she felt the laugh go away. He cousin John beside her was trying to make her look at him. She knew the laugh would come back so she stared straight at the bald spot on the back of Uncle Wally's head.

Uncle Wally called her Sunshine and always wanted her to sit on his lap at family reunions. Fiona hoped he'd ask Deborah this time when they gathered at Aunt Ethel's for lunch after the funeral. At family dinners Uncle Hank's bottle of rye was allowed out of the garage to sit beside Aunt Ethel's bottle of medicinal sherry on the kitchen table all afternoon.

It was hot in the hall. Fiona felt the back of her legs stick to the seat of the chair. She was hungry.

This was the most interesting summer she had ever had 'back home' as father called it.

Every summer Mother and Father took a private vacation and Fiona got to know the family. In exchange for taking her in, Aunt Ethel had free reign to educate Fiona in how to live a Christian life. "Saving your soul," Aunt Ethel told her, "for the final judgement."

"You've come at a bad time this year girl. It's our trip to the city in two days. If we can't find something for you to do while we're gone, you'll just have to come."

On Friday Aunt Ethel, Aunt Hilda, and Aunt Margaret dressed in their best Sunday dresses. All had curled their gray hair, all had put on lipstick and perfume from Avon except for Aunt Hilda who wore Evening in Paris.

Fiona could spot Avon anywhere. Brenda's mom was an Avon lady. Brenda, Shelly, and Fiona used to cut out pictures of perfume and bubble bath bottles from the Avon books and arrange them on their dressers. Now that they were older Brenda's mom gave them lipstick samples. Salmon Pink, Cotton Candy, Poppy Red, Fiona knew all the lipstick colours the Aunts wore.

Aunt Hilda bustled past Fiona on the way to the washroom. Fiona took a deep breath. She liked the smell of Aunt Hilda.

"Have to use the washroom Ethel, don't want to be stuck in an awkward situation on the bus. Make sure you go before we leave Fiona." She winked at her.

"Uncle Hank's waiting," Fiona called. She watched out the kitchen window as he backed the car out of the garage.

Before they left Aunt Ethel led them all in a prayer praising the beautiful day and asking for the Lord's guidance and protection in their travels.

Uncle Hank drove them to SAM'S SERVICE STATION to wait for the bus. She sat in the car with him while her aunts went in to buy their tickets.

"Now don't let the girls get into trouble today," he said with a smile on his face. "Here comes the dog now, off you go."

"Better sit by the window or you'll be squirming the two hours it takes to get there." Aunt Ethel ushered Fiona to the seats just behind the driver. Aunt Hilda and Aunt Margaret sat across the aisle. Fiona watched out the bus window, counted blue cars and listened to the Aunts' talking. They were going first to Kresges, then to the fair, then to get some Chinese food for supper.

"Too bad we don't have a Chinaman anymore."

"He never went to Church anyway."

"Every town is supposed to have a Chinaman."

"Kresge's has plastic tablecloths on sale."

"And work socks."

"And cotton days of the week underwear."

"Not going to church didn't affect the quality of his food any."

"My, my, it's so hot I've lost track of what town this is."

Fiona watched as more people boarded the bus. The bus was stopped outside of a restaurant called THE IMPERIAL CAFE CHINESE AND CANADIAN. All the ladies had their hair done and wore lipstick. Just like the Aunts thought Fiona. She wondered if Kresge's was their magic store too and if they were going to the city to buy plastic tablecloths. Aunt Ethel had quite a collection with checks, flowers, and polka dots. If it was Sunday dinner she used one of her crocheted tablecloths and covered it with a clear piece of plastic. Fiona had put a hot pot on the plastic once. She felt her face turn red remembering Aunt Ethels reaction. She just wasn't used to them. Mother never used tablecloths.

Fiona had counted 50 blue cars and had seen a license plate from Texas by the time the bus pulled into the depot in the city. The Aunts exchanged their latest recipes and household hints during the last two hours and set off for Kresge's as soon as they left the bus. Fiona followed behind.

Even from the back they look like sisters she thought noticing their skirts swished in unison and their purses dangled from the same arm. Just like grandma used to.

Once in the store Fiona walked up and down the housewares and linen aisle. If I had all the money in the world and my own house I would choose one of everything here except those orange towels, thought Fiona. She especially liked a set of china coffee mugs with pink roses on them.

She bought postcards to send to Brenda and Shelley. Aunt Ethel bought two tablecloths. Aunt Margaret bought work socks for Uncle Wally, and Aunt Hilda winking bought Fiona the underwear on sale and for herself a shade of lipstick the Avon lady didn't have, even though Aunt Margaret thought she did.

Over soup and toast at the Kresge's lunch counter Aunt Ethel said it was vain the way she had five shades already and God would probably have found her a husband if she was just a little more humble.

Fiona watched the two waitresses whispering behind their hands. She felt her face turn red again. They had been doing that since Aunt Ethel had folded her hands and fervently gave thanks for the bowl of tomato rice soup the waitress had placed in front of her. Fiona stared into her bowl and refused the piece of raisin pie that came for desert. The aunts split it three ways.

"Can't waste food you've paid money for dear," said Aunt Margaret putting a fork full into her mouth.

Fiona wished Uncle Hank would magically appear in the door of Kresge's and take them all back home. She was glad when the aunts rose to pay their bill and leave.

Going to the fair with the aunts wasn't as much fun as going with Brenda and Shelly, or even mother and father. Mother liked the Ferris wheel at least. Father was wonderful at the duck shoot. He said Aunt Hilda taught him. Fiona was shocked to realize the only thing the aunts were really interested in was whether or not Mrs. Stewart won the quilting competition for the fifth year in a row. Not one of the aunts had ever met her but they followed her awards at fairs and competitions the way Uncle Hank and Father followed the Toronto Maple Leafs and the Boston Bruins.

"Well, Well." Aunt Ethel beamed with pride.

"Must be a record," exclaimed Aunt Margaret.

"The paper might print her picture this year," Aunt Hilda offered.

"Want to try the Duck Shoot Aunt Hilda?" Fiona was getting into the spirit of the fair. People were walking by with big smiles and cotton candy. She could hear the music from the Merry Go Round over the screams of the people on the Tilt-a-Whirl. "Step right up!" yelled the man in the Duck Shoot booth. The sound of the announcer from the race track drifted over the fair goers "And their off.."

The women were silent after Fiona's request. Aunt Ethel and Aunt Margaret looked at Aunt Hilda, eyebrows raised.

"Hilda?" Aunt Ethel asked.

Uh-oh. Fiona thought.

"How nice of you to ask dear, but my aim isn't as good as it once was. Besides, we won't have time if we want supper and to catch the bus."

Aunt Margaret and Aunt Ethel were still looking at Hilda.

"Doesn't anyone think it is too hot to be standing out here?" she asked fanning herself with an envelope she pulled out of her handbag.

"Well. Yes. Indeed," Aunt Ethel mumbled, checked her watch with a frown and announced they should all be going.

"No rides?" asked Fiona.

"No rides." Aunt Ethel had heard on the CBC news someone had been hurt on a ride in Vancouver and she wasn't going to be responsible for any injury to her brother's child.

"Besides, you're wearing a dress. It wouldn't be ladylike."

You could say a prayer since yours work so well, Fiona thought to herself feeling disappointed.

The aunts were ogling over a little baby in a stroller as they waited for a taxi to take them to the Canton Gardens.

Must be the gray hair thought Fiona checking her watch. Three thirty. Four hours until the bus. This is the longest day of my life, thought Fiona.

"Four number one combination plates and four Coke-a-colas" Aunt Ethel was ordering. Her mouth was set in a straight line. She was not pleased that Aunt Margaret went to the liquor store across the street. Her bottle of sherry was low

"You never know when I'll get back to the city," Aunt Margaret blurted.

Aunt Ethel leveled her most disapproving stare at her younger sister.

"Margaret's sherry always seems to disappear faster than Ethels," Mother noted after one family visit.

"She's always been sickly you know," Father replied with a smile.

"I wondered." Mother said.

Aunt Margaret returned just as Fiona noticed the waiter heading toward their table, plates in both hands. Remembering lunch at Kresge's she excused herself and headed for the washroom.

She put her face close to the mirror, stuck her tongue out at herself. She said Aunt Ethels grace inside her head. "Come Lord Jesus be our guest, and to us this food be blessed." She flushed the toilet and washed her hands. When she returned to the table the Aunts were eating.

Good timing she thought. Everyone finished their meal in silence. Aunt Ethel declined fortune cookies for them all.

"Nonsense," she declared. "Dabbling with the occult is a sin."

The aunts divided the bill three ways and Aunt Hilda left a quarter for the tip.

"Don't see why," Aunt Ethel complained. "He's making a wage." She tucked a pair of unused chopsticks into her big black purse.

"Thank-you very much for dinner," Fiona told her aunts.

Aunt Hilda pressed a fortune cookie into her hand as they walked out of the door. Fiona quickly put it in her purse.

They left the restaurant and walked the five blocks to the bus depot.

"Ah," said Aunt Hilda once they got there. "A place to sit." She collapsed on the bench and closed her eyes.

Fiona looked at the clock and groaned inside. Two hours until the bus comes. She walked around the bus depot. Read the covers of every magazine at the newsstand. She walked by the restaurant and then read the headlines on the newspapers in the newsstand. She walked back to the benches in the waiting area and sat with Aunt Margaret. Aunt Ethel was reading DAILY INSPIRATIONS and Aunt Margaret was reading the newspaper. Aunt Hilda was resting. Fiona waited for Aunt Margaret to finish the paper so she could read the cartoons. She watched the red second hand go around the clock a few times. She watched the people in the bus station come and go. There were buses arriving and leaving, drivers in grey uniforms having coffee when they weren't taking tickets and helping people on the bus.

"Remember little Gordie that lived on the corner?" Aunt Margaret asked.

"Hmm," Aunt Ethel looked up from her book. "What about him?"

'His daughter just graduated from Nursing School. Hilda didn't you date him once?"

Aunt Ethel looked at Hilda. "TCH," she said shaking her head. "Let's wake her up and get some coffee. We have an hour before the bus comes."

"Hilda," she said shaking her. Aunt Hilda's purse fell to the floor. "Come Hilda we're going to get a cup of coffee before the bus comes."

Aunt Ethel bent over her. "Margaret," she said sharply, come help me." Fiona was puzzled. Aunt Ethel didn't look too good. She whispered to Aunt Margaret. Aunt Margaret didn't look too good either.

"Help me get her to the washroom," she said. "Fiona bring Hilda's purse."

With one arm over each shoulder Aunt Margaret and Aunt Ethel made their way to the washroom. Aunt Hilda's feet dragged on the ground. Fiona held the washroom door open while Aunt Margaret and Aunt Ethel sat her on the floor against the wall.

"Margaret, I think she's dead."

Fiona's stomach felt like it was on the roller coaster. Her hands were sweaty. She wished Uncle Hank would walk through the door of the washroom right now and take them all home. She felt tears in her eyes. Fiona wished mother and father were back from their vacation. She watched Aunt Ethel trying to find signs of life, a heart beat, breathing, they kept calling Aunt Hilda's name and patting her cheeks. Both looked pale.

"I'll go phone the men," Aunt Margaret took her purse and left the washroom.

Aunt Ethel began to pray. She was on her knees, hands clasped together, eyes closed and face lifted towards heaven. Fiona watched her lips moving.

"Aunt Margaret is taking a long time," she said.

She wanted Aunt Ethel to stop praying and do something. Now Aunt Ethel looked like a Y with her arms open and held above her shoulders. If anyone walks in here I'll be so embarrassed, Fiona thought. She stared at Aunt Hilda while Aunt Ethel asked the Lord to receive her sister's soul; to be by the side of her friends and family during this time of difficulty and to send a sign she could use as guidance for getting Hilda home.

Aunt Hilda doesn't look any different, Fiona thought. She looked up at the ceiling of the washroom to see if she could see signs of the Lord the way it seemed Aunt Ethel could. The washroom had a bare light bulb and three globs of pink bubble gum were stuck to the ceiling above the sink. If she looked up she could almost pretend she was somewhere else.

Aunt Margaret bustled in.

"No one is answering their phones at home, even Wally! I called Susan to find out what was going on. The Church is burning. All the men are out fire fighting."

Aunt Ethel groaned, "You didn't tell her what happened?"

"Of course not."

"What are we going to do?" asked Fiona.

"We could call a funeral home here in the city," said Aunt Ethel.

"We'd have to call the police first," said Aunt Margaret. "and we'll miss the bus and have to stay the night. Hilda's ticket will be wasted."

"Margaret! Give me your sherry."

Aunt Ethel sprinkled Aunt Hilda with half the bottle taking care not to get any on herself. "No sense wasting the bus ticket, the men will help us when we get back."

Fiona stared at Aunt Ethel in amazement, "We're taking her on the bus?"

"Everyone will think she's drunk and sleeping it off. Close your mouth girl before a fly decides to land in there. I'll sit beside her."

Aunt Ethel and Aunt Margaret dragged Aunt Hilda back to the same bench she was sitting on before. People kept giving Aunt Hilda nasty looks now that she smelled so strong of sherry. She could see the condemnation in their eyes. She's not really like this Fiona wanted to yell. What if some of these people know her? Fiona felt so sad, so afraid to say anything.

Fiona leaned against the wall of the bus. She put her forehead against the cool window. She didn't count cars. In the window reflection she could see Aunt Hilda and the man sitting beside her. Aunt Ethel couldn't believe their luck when a raggedy old man smelling as strong of stale whiskey as her sister did of fresh sherry befriended the silent Hilda. He staggered over to her bench and fell beside her.

"Hey Sweetheart," he nudged Hilda in the side with his elbow. "Wanna know what I have in my pocket? Heh, heh, heh. We could have a little fun you and I."

Aunt Ethel and Aunt Margaret sat straight looking stern until the bus arrived.

"Hilda." Ethel took one of her shoulders, Margaret took the other. "Its time to go home."

"Leave her with me!" The man grinned I'm on that bus too. I'll take good care of her." His teeth were brown and a few were missing.

"Fiona, make sure you have Hilda's purse."

"Ladies, Ladies," the stinking old man said. "Let me give you a hand. This fine woman and I understand each other well. A friend in need, is a friend indeed. We've both been here before. Come on lass," he said and hoisted Aunt Hilda like she was a bag of flour over his shoulder and carried her onto the bus.

Fiona could hear the old man with the brown teeth telling Aunt Hilda dirty jokes and laughing at his own humour. She looked at Aunt Ethel beside her. The older woman was looking straight ahead, hands clasped together on her lap. Fiona patted Aunt Ethel's hands.

"Its okay Auntie, it'll all work out, we're almost home."

Fiona thumbed through the post cards she bought Brenda and Shelly then remembered the fortune cookie Aunt Hilda gave her. She opened it and took out the slip of paper. YOUR SMILE WILL BRING YOU GREAT RICHES it read. She put everything back in her purse and leaned her head against the window again and watched Aunt Ethel's reflection in the window until the bus stopped at SAMS SERVICE STATION. There was Uncle Hank ready to help them all off the bus.

The minister was just finishing the funeral service.

"Go in peace to love and serve the Lord."

The organist began playing Amazing Grace as the Uncles filed to the front to carry Hilda to the waiting hearse out by the front door. After they passed, Aunt Ethel leaned over to Fiona.

"Do you smell it too?"

"Smell what Auntie?"

"Perfume," she said. "Evening in Paris."

*   *   *

Deborah was making faces at Fiona when Uncle Wally called her over. "Go on Fiona," Father said, "you have to show respect for your elders."

They had just arrived for the family reunion. There were hellos and hugs and oh my goodnesses all over the place. Sometimes Fiona was safe and didn't have to kiss the uncles hello. It depended on how many beers they drank by the time she arrived with father and mother, or how many of them were already there. The uncles all sat in a circle in Aunt Ethel's backyard on green webbed lawnchairs or chairs from Aunt Ethel's kitchen around one open case of beer and a whole bunch of empty ones. As the day went on, the empties grew but always there was an open case of beer. The Aunts all sat in another circle around the picnic table, or in the kitchen with Grandma. Fiona and her cousins ran around the back yard making up names for each other, playing tag, and seeing how many pieces of water-melon, Mennonite sausage, and Grandma's sugar buns they could eat.

Uncle Wally had wet lips, shiny pink lips, that spit when he talked. He was always wiping his lips with his shirt sleeves. Uncle Wally smelled like beer and Aqua Velva and cigarettes. He gave big wet kisses right on the lips or on the cheek. Then he'd ruffle Fiona's hair, call her sunshine and tell her what a good girl she was and how much she'd grown since last summer while Fiona wiped the kiss off her lips and the spit off her cheek. Uncle Wally would call her over later for another kiss and tell her she was his favorite. He'd do the same to Debra, and Leanne, and Vivian, or any of the girl cousins. If any of the Aunts came by serving food to the men he'd do the same to them. He made them sit on his lap and held his arms tight around their waists.

Fiona respectfully moved around the circle getting more wet kisses and pats on the head and moved on to the Aunts before finding Deborah and the rest of her cousins. They ended the day roasting marshmallows and making up names for the uncles. Uncle Movie Star, Uncle Professor, Uncle Preacher, Uncle Lips.

*   *   *

"Frankly, I'm getting quite tired of this game," Jaqueline said outloud. She looked around in surprise. It wasn't often she talked to herself. Outloud anyway. She was quite careful not to. This was the first sign, her mother told her, of going crazy. She put her deck of cards away, the fancy ones Fiona and Robert gave her for Christmas. They had no more wins in them than the cheap Bicycle cards from Zellers. She told Fiona too.

"It was just a waste of money getting those hoi poloi cards, can't win any more than I usually do. Did you think the gilt edge would bring more luck?"

"No I just thought you'd like something nice for your nightly session of solitaire. It was only supposed to make you feel a little bit special."

"I feel special when I win. Don't need a lousy fancy deck of cards to do that."

Jesus that girl has strange ideas. She probably thinks I have only new lacy underwear, fancy pj's, feminine sheets and expensive bubble bath just to make myself feel better. Nightly pampering is the consolation prize for not having a man to go to bed with. I would need new underwear in that case thought Jaqueline, thinking of the dresser drawer with the worn faded underwear, no one to see me in them, why should I get new until I absolutely need it.

Midnight. She flipped through the tv channels three times before turning it off. The silence closed in on her. She turned on the radio but couldn't decide if she should listen to country, middle of the road or rock and roll, settled on a talk show out of Denver. American Politics. Ah well, at least it's other human voices and conversation of a sort.

Yes she was lonely. She missed not so much Peter she told herself, but the kinds of companionship you got from being part of a couple. One day last week she was having coffee with a friend and watched a woman at another table put her hand on her husbands arm and stroked it up and down. Jaqueline's eyes flooded with tears, there was an ache in her arms. I don't have the right to do that to anyone.

She got up from the couch and looked at the ads she clipped from the paper and put by the phone. It was the third day in a row she looked at them and just couldn't phone. What if all they want is sex? Do you kiss on the first date in the nineties when you're in your 60's?

Carefully she put the ads in her wallet. There she wouldn't lose them and there would be no possibility of Fiona finding them and teasing her. This way she won't be able to look at me with that smug self righteous I-told-you-so glint in her eyes.

Jaqueline made her way back to the couch. Changed the station on the radio.

"Hi, this is Dr. Laura"

Jaqueline turned off the radio and unplugged it. She bundled it up under her arm and set it up on her bedside table, plugged it in and crawled into bed. She turned the light off and listened in the dark the voices keeping her company, other peoples problems made hers seem so slight. Half the women who called in wouldn't have the troubles they call about if their mothers had taught them the manners of a lady. She snuggled down into the blankets and waited for sleep or the morning whichever came first.

* * *

It is true thought Jaqueline, there really is magic. The northern lights display are just for this night. Peter and Jaqueline are driving the twenty miles home after celebrating their fifteenth anniversary at the La Verendre Motel Restaurant. It is August and Jaqueline has the window rolled down, her head out the window watching the changing pattern of the northern lights. Sometimes she turns her head the wrong way and the wind takes her breath away. The whole day has been perfect. Even the songs on the radio seem to be chosen for their anniversary.

Peter had flowers delivered to her during the afternoon, took her out for steak dinner, presented her with a new diamond ring and now they were on their way home to kill the bottle of champagne in the fridge. Jaqueline planned to continue the celebration in bed. She would wear her latest enticement: the blue see through pair of shorty pj's she ordered from Eaton's last month when the baby bonus cheque came. She had fallen in love with the scalloped lace hem and the bows on the shoulders and decided it reminded her of her wedding cake. It was quite the risky item to order from the Eaton's catalogue. Susan worked at the catalogue office and would tell everyone what Jaqueline had planned for her anniversary celebration.

Jaqueline watched Peter as he drove. Such a handsome man she thought.

"So," he said I can hardly wait to see the negligee you ordered from the catalogue that everyone is teasing me about."

Jaqueline sighs with contentment.

"What a good day today was," she says and giggles because she had drank just enough. Peter looks at her smiles, and sings along with Johnny Mathis on the radio. *Until the twelfth of never, I'll still be loving you.*

* * *

Fiona turned on her reading light. Should she read or knit? She tried to peer out the window to see what was out there. Just dark. It was close to 2 a.m. The bus was somewhere between Kamloops and Jasper. Probably coming up to Blue River. She knew the mountains were out there. Gray rock, green trees, some white snow near the tips and on the north sides where the sun doesn't get to often. Night. Fiona pictured the bus in her mind, flying over the miles all dark except for the headlights and the reading light in the window where she sat.

* * *

Father is driving the black Plymouth over the gravel roads to his favorite fishing spot. Fiona bounces around in the back seat. She's trying to float free form to see if the road will bounce her between the two door windows as the car lurches around potholes and bounces on washboard roads. Periodically she cheats and influences the direction of the bounce.

There are tiger lillies blooming in the ditches. Mother will pick a bouquet on the way home. She'll put them in the big crystal vase and place it on the dining room table. Fiona can hear the fishing tackle jingle in the trunk.

Mother sits in the front seat clinging to the picnic lunch she made while father and Fiona ate breakfast. She doesn't want the lemonade to spill all over the front seat.

"Please, Peter don't drive so fast over the bumps."

Father laughs and takes a drink of beer from the bottle he's hidden in an old black sock.

There is a day like this every summer, Fiona thinks, as the three of them parade lawn chairs, fishing rods and tackle, picnic lunch in a brown paper bag, and a blanket for Jaqueline to suntan on. The Tan Too mosquito repellent is in the bag with the picnic lunch. It takes two trips along the footpath through the trees before everything they need is at father's favorite fishing spot, a large rocky platform surrounded by bush. There is another group fishing about 50 yards off to the left. Father starts swearing.

Jaqueline spreads the blanket out on the rock and places the bag with their picnic lunch in the shade of a rocky outcrop.

"Hmm," says father to Jaqueline, "Bikini weather." He gives her a pinch on her behind. Fiona is mortified, she is the only kid in school with a mother who wears bikinis.

For hours they cast their lines, hook fish that get away, catch snags on the lake bed and drag up bright green weeds from the bottom. Finally the fish start biting and whenever they haul one in father hits it over the head with the pair of pliers from his tackle box. Fiona squirms inside. She can't understand how he can touch the fish. She's revolted by the sight of the gills, opening and closing, drowning in air, the way humans do in water but with eyes that never close. She figures it takes ten minutes for them to die. The fish Fiona catches with the red and white spoon thrashes on the rock. Father hits it with the pliers twice. Father tries Fiona's gear and catches another pike. Mother lands two pickerel with just plain baited hooks.

On the way home Jaqueline picks her bouquet of lillies, they eat the last of the picnic lunch in the car careful not to get too many sandwich crumbs on the red seats.

When they get home Mother and Fiona cart everything except the fish into the house. Father is seated at the table preparing to clean the fish. He's covered the table with twelve layers of newspaper. There are four fish lined up on his left hand side, an empty platter on his right and the garbage can on the floor next to his left leg. As he sharpens the knife he insists Fiona sit opposite him so she can see what he's doing in case there is ever a time she needs to clean fish. "Like when," Fiona asks, hand on her hip, eyes rolling at mother.

"Well if ever you're in a plane that crashes near a lake you'll be able to catch fish and cook them for dinner. You won't starve and you won't have to eat the passengers that died."

"Oh God," says Fiona, "that's gross."

Father has also insisted that she learn how to put oil in a car, and change a flat tire. Things she needs to know in case of dire emergencies.

Father begins to sharpen his knife. Fiona gets goose bumps on her arms as the knife is stroked against the steel. She watches as he works to a rhythm, one two, one two, one two. Fiona looks at the fish lying on the table. She knows she will never be able to sit through this whole ritual. She never has. Its a ceremony repeated every summer. Over the years she's caught enough parts of it. She has it all memorized.

Father begins by cutting off their heads one at a time. He uses a sawing motion to cut through the bony part of the neck. Blood starts flowing. This is where Fiona usually leaves. It reminds her too much of the stories in Aunt Ethel's bible about sacrificing lambs.

Today Fiona just turns away and watches out the window until she hears father crumple up the first layer of newspaper. She knows the paper will be blotted with dark red blood, the way her Kotex pads are when she has her period, or the way bandages are when they cover up a bad cut. After he throws it into the garbage, she can look. He slits the belly, a mass of orange fish eggs spill out onto the newspaper. Fiona shivers. Father reaches in with his fingers, takes out the guts, plops them into the garbage along with the eggs. Father crumples another layer of newspaper and throws it away. He skins the fish, cuts off fillets and piles them onto the waiting platter.

Father starts cutting up another fish. He asks Fiona if she wants to take over.

"No," she says quietly looking away.

Father has stopped with his knife half way through the first cut. Blood pours onto the newspapers.

"You can take over Fiona," he says firmly, pushing his chair away from the table, leaving the knife where he stopped cutting.

"No," Fiona says quietly. The backs of her knees are tingling. Her mouth is dry, her hands are sweating. Father forces her onto the chair. Takes her small hands in his huge ones, places her left hand on the cold clammy fish, puts her right hand on the knife, begins sawing through the bones, the flesh, more blood seeps into the newspapers. Fiona's stomach heaves with the first crunch through bone. The smell of vomit mixes with the smell of fish blood.

"Jesus Christ!" father yells, crumples the newspaper around the rest of the fish and throws them into the garbage.

* * *

Fiona was looking over the bus schedule she picked up in Kamloops. The bus was due for a 6 a.m. arrival in Edmonton. The City of Champions. Football, hockey, even baseball. All the sports Robert hated, all the sports Fiona loved.

Father would take her to Taylor Field once during summer holidays, even took her to Flin Flon Bomber games. She still had an autographed stick.

"Come here Fiona, I'd like you to meet some friends of mine. This is Bobby Clarke, Reggie Leach, Murray Anderson."

"She sure is better looking than you." People always said that. Usually fathers friends said that. It was some kind of banter she never understood the reason for, all of it cliches.

"How's the weather up there?"

"How goes the battle?"

"Hey you old rooster, how's the old lady?"

By now they were between Jasper and Edmonton. The sun was beginning to rise. Fiona was looking forward to the hour stop in the city, a break from the drone and vibration of the bus motor. She felt as if she were passing through some ordeal, travelling all night with her demons.   Her head was full of echoes:

"Get out of here, get out of here."

"I'm not afraid of you anymore."

"Can't you wear your hair more attractively than that?"

" She sure is better looking than you."

"A lady never runs in a dress."

"Hey princess, want to go to a game?"

" If I'm not there to meet your bus I don't want anything to do with you."

"Nothing to do with you."

The voices rang in her head the way church bells pealed calling the faithful to worship. Over and over:

"Get out of here."

"That's not ladylike."

"Are you alright?"

"Want to go to a game?"

"A game."

"Get out of here."

A lady probably doesn't cry in public. Thought Fiona.

*   *   *

"Get away from me, shithead!"

Fiona was trying to dipsy doodle away from Bob. They had been playing street hockey since just after supper. The score was 10-10. The street
light by Doug's house created an umbrella of light making the boundary of
their playing area a circle. It was Fiona, Kenny, and Doug against Phil,
Bobby, and Gary.

"Fiona your Mom's here," Phil said as he picked the puck off her stick.
He dodged Kenny, stick handling his way to where Gary stood with his
goalie stick protecting a space between two coffee cans filled with ice
near the edge of the light circle.

Fiona turned to look. There she was. Navy parka unzipped, slippers on
her feet, no gloves and her arms were moving up and down like crow's
wings in summer. Caw caw caw thought Fiona watching Jaqueline's mouth
move up and down not hearing the words. She took off her toque.

"Come here Fiona, right this minute."

I could run...straight down this street to the highway and on and on.
She knew she was in trouble. She walked to her mother.

"Fiona Louise, that was no way for a lady to talk! I knew as soon as I
saw you out here playing hockey again you'd be using strong language. A
lady doesn't curse. Get in the house right now. You're too old to play with
boys! Put that stick down and go finish your homework."

Fiona looked at Jaqueline. How did I ever end up with her as a mother
she wondered looking at how green her skin appeared in the streetlight.
She looked like an old martian with her face screwed up in the disap-
proval look, her mouth coloured with Avon's Poppy Red lipstick. The white
vapor from her hot breath hitting the outside air evaporated above her
head the way the cigarette smoke dissipated in air. Fiona watched as it
floated above and disappeared against the dark sky. The sour smell of
Jacqueline's breath wafted towards her.

"Phil," Fiona raised her voice, "Thanks for the stick."

"See you tomorrow Fiona"

"Yeah, see you."

Fiona shoved the butt end into the snowbank and turned to follow her
mother home. She heard the boys giggle and a falsetto "Ladies don't talk
like that." Then more laughter. She had never felt so embarrassed in her
life.

"Really Fiona, girls don't play hockey and you shouldn't play with boys
anymore. What are people like Mr. and Mrs Baker going to think?" Jaqueline
opened the door and let Fiona walk into the house before her.

"Mom, I was just playing hockey."

"But that will lead to other things and you'll get a reputation for being fast. Ladies don't hang around with boys and they don't talk the way I heard you speak out there. You're grounded for a week. No staying with Brenda on the weekend."

"Mom, that's not fair. There is nothing to do in the house in the winter." Fiona took off her parka and hung it in the closet, then put her mitts on the hot air register so they would be dry in the morning.

"Fiona shut your mouth and don't talk back. The boys won't have respect for you if you play hockey with them. In the end when all is said and done they won't treat you like a lady-they'll be too familiar and you won't have any mystique. Besides I don't want you hanging around with that Phil. He's trouble, I hear." Her eyes narrowed, "What else has been happening out there?"

"Nothing."

I hope none of them have tried to kiss you."

"Mom! We just play hockey."

"No more. I forbid you to play. No daughter of mine is going to hang around boys and ruin her reputation. Now get to your room. I don't want to see you anymore tonight. And don't forget you're grounded."

The next morning it was still dark when Fiona walked to the bus stop. Kenny, Bobby, Phil, and Doug were huddled in a circle smoking.

"Fiona," Phil said and nodded.

"Did you catch shit last night?" Kenny asked.

"A bit," she said, "Look, I'm really sorry. But, uh, is the big game against George and his gang still on Sunday night?"

"THE BUS IS COMING, THE BUS IS COMING." Bobby's little brother David yelled. The boys dropped their smokes and passed around a pack of Wrigleys Doublemint before Mr. Butcher could catch them smoking.

"Uh, yeah," said Doug looking at the ground. "But we don't want you to play anymore. You're Mom makes trouble for us with our folks. Sorry."

"You're good for a girl," said Kenny, "And maybe we need another player, but we can't have your mom stoping the game on Sunday."

Fiona could hardly see the steps of the bus when she climbed aboard. She felt foolish with her eyes full of tears. Blindly she found her friend Brenda, who always saved her a seat.

"You're lucky to have the same bus stop as Phil. He's so cute. Can you come to my house and do homework tonight?"

"No. I'm grounded."

"What did you do?"

"Nothing. Just played hockey. I think she heard me swearing."

"Mothers are B-I-T-C-H-es." said Brenda. "Look at the ugly pants mine made me wear."

Fiona pressed the tip of her index finger on the frosty bus window and watched as a clear space melted. She blew on it until it was large enough to look out of and watched the trees and buildings go by. She looked out the window, making her peephole bigger and bigger while the high school girls sang their repertoire of Petula Clark's Downtown, Found a Peanut, Diana Ross and Nancy Sinatra.

Fiona sang quietly along with them.

'These boots are made for walking,
and that's just what they'll do
One of these days these boots are gonna
walk all over you. "

Fiona thought this was a funny song. On the Ed Sullivan Show, Nancy Sinatra was wearing white go-go boots and everyone on the bus was wearing brown or black snow boots. She pictured snow boots possessed by the devil walking by themselves over people.

"Brenda, do you over feel like running away?" Fiona turned from the window.

"Yeah, when my Mom's a real bitch and it seems like I can't do anything right."

The bus pulled up to Scott Junior High.

"See you after school," Brenda said as they climbed off the bus.

Fiona stood where the bus left them and watched as Phil and the boys and Brenda and the rest of the kids walked into the school. She looked down the road. I could just walk and walk and walk and keep going on and on forever. No one would miss me. She looked across the street at the Arena.

"Girls don't play hockey. It's unladylike to sweat," she mimicked. "Ladies wear dresses, why do you want to wear those pants? Keep your knees together..."

The buzzer rang. She turned and ran for the front doors of the school.

"Hey Dad, wouldn't it be great to play in the NHL?"

Fiona and Peter were making popcorn. It was Saturday night. Hockey Night in Canada was on tv. Peter was pouring melted butter over the bowl of popped corn.

"Its nice to know I have a date every Saturday night in the winter," Peter winked at her.

Fiona just grinned and handed Peter his rye and Coke. She took a sip of her orange juice.

"Where's the rooster?" he asked."

"Who?"

"The rooster...your mother."

Fiona stared, puzzled, at Peter.

"Don't you think she reminds you of a rooster in the morning with her hair standing on end and all that crowing?"

Fiona laughed. "I thought she was like a crow."

"Not with that hair." Peter downed half his drink and topped it up with rye. "Come on let's go watch the game. Boston and Toronto, my girl."

"Boston's my favorite team." Fiona sat on the floor in front of the television.

"Is Bobby Orr your favorite hockey player?"

"No. Derek Sanderson."

"Aahh, he's a goon."

"Oh Dad! He's real cute, and when he skates his hair blows behind him. Brenda thinks he's cute too. Shelly likes Bobby Orr but Brenda and I think he's too baby-faced."

"Peter really you shouldn't be encouraging her about this hockey business."

"Hey Jackie what' the big deal? A lot of women like hockey."

"She wants to play."

"Its impossible for girls to play so don't worry about it. Leave the girl alone. There's no harm done."

"YES! Cheevers stopped him," Fiona cheered.

"Fiona! Don't yell in the house," Jaqueline spoke firmly as she zipped up her jacket.

"Say hello to Joyce for me. Look at him move! Baby face or not Fiona you're looking at history."

"Oh, for heavens sake, I'll be home when I'm home."

Both Fiona and Peter erupted in cheers.

"One nothing for us Dad."

Fiona heard her mother close the outside door.

"Hey Dad, wouldn't it be great to play in the NHL? Heck, I'd be happy just to play hockey here in the Memorial Arena. I love the sounds and the smell of the ice."

"Girls can't play hockey," Peter said gently. "Street hockey is one thing, forget about the arena."

"I wish I were a boy," Fiona said quietly.

"Come now, I don't," Peter said.

"But then you wouldn't tell me to hush and not think about it when I tell you how hard I imagine what it feels like skating fast down the ice, hair blowing behind you and Foster Hewit saying, 'He's split the defense. He shoots, he scores! What a fine play ladies and gentlemen.' Why is it wrong to imagine?"

"Give it up princess, it won't get you anywhere. Pay attention to the game now."

Fiona opened her eyes and stared at the ceiling. She heard the Baker's car start. Fiona looked at her alarm clock. 10:00, must be time for Church. Sunday. Fiona felt knife-like stabs in her stomach. The day of the big game and she couldn't play. She rolled on her stomach burying her face in the pillow hoping she could go back to sleep and wake up on Monday, hockey game over and she wouldn't even ask who won.

"Fiona don't be a lazy bones, Get out of bed," Jaqueline called just outside her door.

"In a minute," she answered.

Fiona rolled herself deeper in her blankets knowing her feet would get cold as soon as she stepped out of bed. She heard the telephone ring.

"Fiona its for you."

"Coming." She got up and ran to the kitchen.

"It's Brenda."

"Hello."

"Fiona, Gary wants to talk with you. He's here...the guys thought your Mom wouldn't let you talk if they phoned so hang on a minute."

"Okay."

"Uh, Fiona?"

"Yeah."

"Is your mom listening?"

"Yeah."

"Just answer yes or no then. We guys thought, you know, like, since this was such a big game and everything, that we should make it real, and have a ref. So we took a vote and even George figured, like, you'd be the best person. Maybe if you're just, you know, reffing your mom wouldn't get so mad hey. So what do you think?"

"Uh, I don't know."

"C'mon Fiona its important, you know that."

"Oh, all right...but its not what I want to do."

"Good. I'll tell Phil."

Sunday was cold all day. Fiona finished the Sunday dinner dishes. She had put her coat and boots by the door. Jaqueline was playing her usual game of Solitaire in the living room. Peter was snoring. The Kraft man was giving a recipe on TV. Fiona put on her coat and as she closed the door on the warmth of the house she could hear the slap slap of Jaqueline's cards and the Kraft man's voice as smooth as the peanut butter he was proclaiming.

Silence. She could hear the slight hum of the electrical meter. She walked down the driveway to the street, snow squeaking under her boots. She saw the guys down the road standing in a group. Waiting for her. This was the showdown.

"Fiona," Phil nodded to her and stepped on his cigarette.

"Okay lets go," said George.

Gary paced out the perimeters of the rink staying within the area of the street lamp.

"You know the rules," Phil said to the guys and handed Fiona the puck. "All we need you for is face offs and running after the puck if it goes out of bounds. We only have two tonight so keep an eye on them."

"Okay." Fiona walked to the centre of the rink. Bobby and Wayne were picked to take the face off. Fiona dropped the puck and the game was under way.

Phil had the first chance to score, but put a wrist shot just wide of the jam cans. Fiona had to run all the way to the Green's house two doors away to retrieve the puck. He had another chance after the next face off, but Raymond caught the puck in his baseball glove. George won the next face off and Fiona had to hex him real hard to make sure he missed his chance. Doug deflected the puck to the Riding's garbage can. It landed in a snow bank. They stopped the game to look for the puck. No one could find it. George reached into his coat pocket and brought out the other puck.

"Intermission between periods." said Phil.

The play went back and forth with no one scoring. Fiona kept wishing she could play instead of Kenny. She was better than him. And she could see that Raymond was weak on his left side. Low and to the left I could score on him she thought as she ran to get the puck. As she brought it back to the guys she heard them talking in the distance.

"Great to have your own little groupie," said George.

"Yeah. Comes in handy when you need someone to get the puck. She'll do anything for us."

"Anything Phil?"

Phil only smiled back.

As Fiona dropped the puck she felt the anger start to burn in her. How could they! She was a hockey player, not a groupie. What was going on?

Bobby misdirected a shot past her feet. It hit the snow bank and careened all the way to her house. She just stood and watched it.

"Hey! Fiona!" the guys started yelling.

She watched them carefully, was going to refuse. Just then she heard Jaqueline's voice yelling in the distance.

"Fiona? FIONA!"

She stared running towards her house.

"Aw geez it's her mother," she heard someone say. She reached the puck and picked it up.

"Here, go see your mother, I'll take it from here," Phil said as he caught up to her.

Fiona silently looked him straight in the eyes, then turned and kept running down the street.

"Hey!" Phil called, "Fiona, get back here."

"Fiona Louise!" she heard her mother's shrill yell behind her.

As she ran her parka hood fell off her head. Fiona ran faster and faster. She was breathing gulps of cold air. She ran as fast as she could. With her hood down, all she could hear was the roar of the wind in her ears. This is what hockey players hear. She thought of the roar of the crowd on Hockey Night in Canada. This is what they hear skating down the ice. She clutched the puck harder in her hand. She knew Phil was behind her. She ran faster and faster to the end of the street, to the baseball field. There was nothing but snow covering it, no one had walked on the field for months. When she reached the edge, Fiona twirled like the discuss throwers she watched on tv once, twice, three times around.

"A spin-a-rama, SHE SHOOTS, SHE SCORES," Fiona yelled as she let go of the puck, watched it arc into the dark winter night.

                        *   *   *

"He's done it to me again! GOD DAMN ASSHOLE!" Jaqueline screamed out loud. She turned the ignition key off, put on the four way blinkers, tucked her winter parka closer around her, and moved the seat of the plymouth back a notch or two and made herself comfortable. As comfortable as you could get in the middle of nowhere in February with all that cold creeping in as soon as the car stopped.

You never know how long you'll have to wait before another car comes by on this lonely highway thought Jaqueline. Ten miles from The Pas, ten miles from the airport. This was the third time this month.

"Yes, Yes," Peter said, "Stop nagging there's enough gas."

She was going to miss parent/teacher interviews. Fiona was in grade ten and on the honour role. It was the socially correct thing to go and hear all the good and bad things about your child at school. The unknown part of your child's life. Jaqueline enjoyed these few moments with the teachers, she tried to glean everything she could about Fiona. The Fiona she didn't know fascinated her. The teachers always told her some remarkable tid bit about her daughters personality.

"She is quite an accomplished debater." That futzy old teacher Fiona had last year told her this amazing detail. Wanted to train her for the Reach For The Top school team. Well, I'll be Jaqueline always said to herself. It was like putting together a jigsaw puzzle, another piece to go here and there and soon the whole picture starts to emerge.

I should've taken Shirley up on her offer to drive and go for a drink at the lounge of the Gateway Hotel. The lounge not the bar.

"C'mon Jaq, we haven't had girls night out since the curling bonspiel." Shirley said after she'd been through a parent/teacher interview for her three daughters she needed a drink for each one of them before she could face their father at home.

Ten minutes and Jaqueline had seen nothing but the dark expanse of highway in front and behind her, no welcome light in the distance growing larger. Jaqueline's toes started to feel the cold nipping through her boots. She took them off and tucked her legs and feet up under her duffel parka.

"Hello Mrs. Loewen," the teacher would say shaking her hand.

"We are very pleased with Fiona's performance to date. There is really nothing for us to talk about, just want to tell you what a pleasant young woman she is. I feel she has a great future in whatever career she wishes to pursue."

"Well thank-you." Jaqueline would reply. " Peter and I are very proud of our daughter." What more could she say, it was all the truth. That would be all the teachers had to say, unless she pushed.

"Does she cause any trouble?"

"No, beyond the odd enthusiastic outburst when the girls are talking."

One teacher sent Fiona to the principal's office for taking a drink from the water fountain out of turn, the principal sent her back to the class-room unscathed, dismissed the crime as being irrelevant. Her daughter was never in danger of the strap or a detention.

Jaqueline had taken her arms out of her coat sleeves and tucked them around her knees inside her parka in an effort to keep her whole body warm.

Running out of things Jaqueline thought.

"Running out of time," she chanted out loud. "Running out of milk, run-ning out of patience, running out of gas, running out of life. With Peter around I run out of things at the most inconvenient times."

Peter and Jaqueline were taking a ride with one of his old school bud-dies. Peter and Curly were in the front of the small airplane, Jaqueline was sitting in the back with Fiona on her lap. Fiona must have been just under a year old. She sat quietly pointing now and then at the pilot and her papa. Curly was a good pilot and flew them all over their favorite places that afternoon, Rocky Lake their fishing spot, Mile 25 where they could make out their neighbours on the beach, the fire rangers station, the house they lived in looked like a drawing in a children's book it was so small from up in the air. Jaqueline remembered thinking that something so small from the air shouldn't take so long to clean.

When they were out over the lake Curly said one of the fuel tanks was empty and he'd have to switch over to the other one. Jaqueline watched while took hold of a lever but it wouldn't budge. She watched him try again. The plane engine became quiet.

"Say your prayers," Curly said. "If I can't get this lever over, we're going down."

They were floating in air, in the bright blue sky, no clouds on the horizon. The lake water looked silver, sparkling in the sunlight. The boats on the water looked like dinky toys, all of them different colours and bobbing on the waves. They reminded Jaqueline of the canoes she made as a child out of pea pods and toothpicks. She would float them in the bathroom sink, create a violent storm with her hand and see how long it would take to sink them.

Jaqueline felt anger inside her. Her baby wasn't even a year old. This was outrageous, this was insulting, why should she have gone to all the trouble of being pregnant and giving birth if this baby was going to die today? She and Peter had at least made it to 25. Who am I supposed to pray to she wondered? God? She held Fiona close to her whispered a quick prayer asking forgiveness for all her faults to any supreme being who was listening and asked if they went down that the baby live.

"I'm so sorry little one." she whispered in Fiona's ear.

Curly gave another tug, the lever moved. Peter wiped his forehead with the hankie he kept in his right hip pocket. Curly managed to get the engines started, looked back at Jaqueline with a grin and asked where she wanted to go now.

Peter, looking very white faced said, "Lets put her down, go home and have a couple of beers with the steaks we were going to barbecue for dinner. It's a nice day, but I'd rather look at the scenery from the ground for a while."

Jaqueline noticed lights in the rear view mirror. She sat up closer and had a good look. Sure enough there was a set of headlights in the distance behind her. Soon a red flashing light appeared and a car pulled in behind her vehicle. The RCMP had arrived on the scene half an hour after the car stopped. It would be Rudy. The same cop who rescued her the other two times.

"Well, Well," he said when Jaqueline rolled down the window after he sauntered over. "Seems you have a perpetual problem, carless operating of a vehicle. Ran out of gas again huh? Tell Peter I'll write him a ticket for putting an unsafe vehicle on the road next time. Or even better I'll make search and rescue charge him mileage and all that if he doesn't get that gas guage fixed. Hop over to the black beast behind you, I have a thermos of coffee in there I'll share with you. I can hear your teeth chattering."

He took care of the details, arranging for a jerry can to be delivered to her here in the middle of nowhere. They drank coffee in the front seat of his police car and gossiped about the jewelry store owner's wife committing suicide, while they waited for the tow truck to bring the gas. Rudy was the cop who responded to the emergency call. It was true he said, she did take an axe to the bathroom mirror before swallowing the bottle of pills. He told her about the high speed chase the other side of town the other day...Joy riding teenagers...their Papas would have to pay a hefty fine.

In the distance they spotted headlights coming closer. "Must be Adam," said Rudy.

Jaqueline was sad. She was enjoying this visit drinking coffee in the front seat staying warm while the winter night closed around the windows and the wind howled around the car. All they could hear in the silent parts of their conversation was the hum of the car motor. If I wasn't married, thought Jaqueline, I could go for a man like Rudy; tall, exciting and competent. I'll bet he never runs out of gas.

Jaqueline was paying the truck driver when Rudy waved good bye, yelled they would have to stop meeting like this and told her he would make Peter buy him a drink the next time he saw him in the bar.

Adam told her there would be just enough to get into town and back home but she'd be running on fumes. Too bad that the gas stations are closed this time of night but If she banged on the boss's door when she got into town, he'd fill 'er up. Jaqueline smiled and thanked him for his trouble. She wasn't going to do a thing. Peter could run out of gas on the next trip to town. She would catch up to Shirley, maybe even Rudy, and collect a few swizzle sticks in the Gateway Hotel for Fiona's collection before coming home.

*   *   *

As soon as she walked into the Edmonton bus station Fiona noticed him. The tall shadow, the movement of hand to mouth, the wisps of cigarette smoke around him. Her body filled with joy. Her arm lifted in a wave her mouth opened and the words "Hey! Dad, over here"were ready, on the tip of her tongue, automatically she was ready to run and leap into the man's arms for a hug. Such a long time it had been, what a relief to see him again, How good it would be, for just a moment to let father take the weight of the world off of her shoulders.

Such strange tricks the mind plays. She remembered just in time. She felt foolish standing there with her arm up and her mouth opened, but no one paid her much attention, people looked for each other all the time in the bus stations.. She walked forward a bit and the image disappeared, there was a man, but he didn't even look like father, shorter, too much hair. A tease was all it was but whose joke? Father had been dead for five years.

*   *   *

Fiona had her bags packed. She was going through her closet one more time to see if there was anything else she should take with her. She was seventeen and leaving home, off to university. Once again mother gave her the lecture about only going out with men who had a chance at a good job. She didn't think Fiona was particularly good university material, but she did approve of her attending for two years at least until she met a man she could marry. Then she could drop out and have children.

"Get your MRS," Mother laughed. Fiona was tired of this joke, mother told it to all of the women she coffeed with, they all giggled too.

Father knocked on her door. When she opened it he stood awkwardly holding a brown paper bag until Fiona invited him in. They sat on the bed. He told her how proud he was of her and how sure he was she would do well in life. Then passed over the paper bag.

"The two most important things you will need in life beyond a good education," he said. Fiona pulled out a cast iron frying pan and a unidriver."

It adapts to fit any kind of screw head your likely to need. You'll never go hungry with a good pan to cook with. You'll be able to fix anything and cook anything, completely independent," He wiped his eyes with the hankie he kept in his pocket and left.

*   *   *

It was summer. Downtown Calgary was all hot concrete and windows. Everything was paralyzed by the heat and wilted under the sun or its reflection. Fiona was going to see father. He was living at the York Hotel in downtown Calgary since he and mother separated. Two nights ago he phoned threatening to kill himself. Take a gun to his head.

"No one would miss me anyway," he said.

Fiona walked passed the trendy shops on the Eighth Avenue mall and kept walking when the mall ended. It was a different downtown now. She passed the pawn brokers a little further along the street. The windows of the building covered in white paper advertising deals in blue and red letters. Fiona turned a corner and passed the orange Triple XXX video store. She turned another corner onto Seventh Avenue. Squished between two other stores was a tiny convenience store, wrought iron fencing protecting its doors and windows. Keeping things in or things out Fiona wondered, looking at an empty newspaper stand in front of the open door. She gritted her teeth. From the small alcove between the convenience store and an ancient tailor shop a puddle of vomit baked in the heat.

"Whew! That's great for business," Fiona mumbled. A little further along she stepped over a puddle. She could see it began with the man asleep on the bench in front of the hotel. A paper bag was clutched in his hand, the leg of his jeans soaked from his crotch to his shoes.

Fiona turned into the doorway of the hotel. The lobby was deserted except for the flies buzzing around the lobby. No air conditioning. She found the stairs and climbed two flights, a hint of stale urine and vomit in the air wafting like perfume. She found room 201. Fiona leaned against the wall. Took a few deep breaths, hand on her chest, she waited for her heart to slow down.

"Made it," she whispered and took another deep breath to steady her nerves and gather enough strength to knock on the door. Fiona only wanted to cry but put her perky daughter smile on her face for the man who would answer the door.

*   *   *

Jaqueline was dreaming of men. They were all sizes and shapes. She was trying to find the perfect man. She had a template with two choices. One was her father, the other was Peter before he started drinking heavily. The ones who almost fit, Jaqueline was holding in a pen on the side, they were supposed to be demonstrating their talents, perhaps some skill they had would make up for the almost but not quiet perfect fit. One fellow was a handy man, she liked him, almost the double of Peter, a little shorter, but he could fix anything. But when she tried to fit him into the father template he wouldn't cooperate.

"Hey lady, you just have to take me as I am. Who says I'll even like you? What if you aren't the perfect woman?"

"But I am perfect," she replies as he jumps over the walls of the pen and jogs away.

"Hey! Come back, there's still a few more men to try before I make my choice."

He looked back over his shoulder and laughed at her. It was Peter's laugh.

"Wait!" she yelled running after him. "Peter wait, come back."

Jaqueline couldn't catch him. She turned and went back to choosing men. She checked on the ones in the pen. Half of them now looked like Peter, the other half like her father.

"Damn, I pressed them too hard through the template"

The ones that looked like Peter started jumping over the walls.

"Your not perfect," they yelled and ran off into the distance.

She opened the pen door and walked in. The men who looked like her father swarmed around her. They all had sad eyes. One by one they patted her on the shoulder.

"Sorry baby," they said.

"Sorry baby," all together

"But I'm perfect," she said to each one of them

"Sorry baby," the chant went on.

"But I'm perfect," she replied.

They chanted again in unison. The refrain sounding like some reply in church. They started mumbling til soon "Sorry baby" sounded like "Amen" and a little gray wizened version of her father appeared.

"Nobody's perfect," he approached her

"Amen," the crowd replied and one by one they disappeared except for the old man.

"Nobody's perfect," he patted her on the shoulder finally and disappeared.

Jaqueline was wandering around the empty pen. In the corner was a pile of old clothes. "Typical of Peter," she said, "To leave a pile of laundry in the corner for me to do"

The clothes began to move slowly taking the shape of a man.

"I snuck in."

"But you didn't fit ."

"It doesn't matter," the man said, his facial features changing...first he was her car mechanic, then the baker, then Beth's husband, the man who sold her house insurance, her doctor, her dentist, the mail man, then every man she ever met. The faces were changing faster and faster. She couldn't keep up with it.

"I think your perfect."

"I think your perfect."

"I think your perfect," the chant went on and on.

*   *   *

When the call came, Fiona said she was on her way.

" I don't think he'll last long," Aunt Ethel said.

Robert was angry that she was going to spend money travelling to see her no good father who was a drunk and lived on skid row and what did he do for us anyway.

Fiona levelled a stare at the ticket agent and asked for a first class seat Vancouver to Calgary and handed over Robert's credit card.

The little man in the hospital bed startled her. 6'5" isn't very tall laying down. The dragon slain. It was pitiful. His skin was the colour of Wrigley's gum when it was chewed too long, and his gray hair had a yellow tinge like the nicotine stained fingers on his right hand or like the old polar bear Fiona saw at the zoo once when she was young. She felt she was betraying him sitting here watching him like this, comparing father then to father now. He looked 84 years old, teeth rotted to the gums, his skull showed through his sagging skin. Fiona counted on her fingers. Yikes she said to herself. He's only 48.

The doctor told her not to expect more than a week.

Father opened his eyes, still blue, though the whites had yellowed. He smiled when he saw her, told her to sit down, he wouldn't bite. She sat in a chair beside his bed in the green hospital room, holding on to the one finger he offered.

"No more walks princess," He said.

She smiled. Tried to keep her face perky so he couldn't read her emotions on her face. Told him it was okay, at least he wouldn't get lost if she held on to him.

They both laughed with tears in their eyes.

"Remember when," father started and kept going all afternoon, story after story, making her laugh.

When the nurses chased her out it was late.

"I'll miss you," he whispered as she kissed his cheek.

She walked down the empty corridor to the elevator, her right foot out at an angle, saying prayers for father.

*   *   *

"You married your mother."

"Pardon?" Fiona snapped out of her inattention. There was a small clay sculpture on the counsellor's desk. Mother and child. A variation on the madonna theme. She was alternately studying this and the embroidered sunflower picture on the wall. Just as the woman said this she was admiring the arrangement of art pieces and books. She was fantasizing about having her own personal reading space. Something she'd always dreamed of....water colours on the wall, a big wing chair surrounded by bookshelves, nice stereo and really flowery wall paper. She wasn't listening to the counsellor. There was Christian literature in the lobby, lots of it. She was wondering if this was really the place for her. Fiona was waiting for the bible quotes and a church schedule when this absurd sentence filtered into her consciousness.

"It seems you've married the same kind of personality your mother has, therefore you encounter the same situations in your marriage as you did in your childhood. You are comfortable with that kind of abuse. You found someone who will give you the same life as you've always known. Breaking the cycle, rebelling, instead of accepting everything would enable self-healing."

*   *   *

Fiona sat on the edge of the examining table swinging her feet. Same room as last time she thought looking down at the paper gown that covered her body. Last time was 2 hours ago. Nothing changed. The jar on the counter still contained two tongue depressors even though she watched a dozen people move through the waiting room. Fiona watched her feet swing back and forth. Heart beat irregularities. Should never have said anything about numb fingers. Now I'll be late and he'll be angry.

Fiona thought her legs sticking out from under the gown looked as purple and mottled in the fluorescent light as the skin of the elderly couple she sat across from in the waiting room. She tried to guess which one was there to see the doctor. There was no way of telling. They touched each other often with hand pats and whispered back and forth. I guess this is what you would call devoted to each other.

She wondered if the fellow who kept looking at his watch was still there. Seeing him fidget and glance at his wrist so often made the wait longer. Really, who has time to be sick. I'll have to get groceries on the way home.

She looked at the posters on the wall. One diagrammed the ear in intimate detail and the other depicted the stages of pregnancy, sponsored by the people who made her birth control pills. What an advertisement.

The ear, the fetal heart, valentine hearts, chocolates in heart boxes. Father was the only man who ever gave her chocolates on Valentines day. Fiona held her breath, she could feel her heart beating. She was nervous. Thump, thump. Nothing irregular to her, steady on, pumping as usual. She let her breath out all at once. Maybe I'll die soon.

Fiona was counting heart beats. She was driving into town with mother and father. They were planning their day. Twenty-eight. Twenty-nine. She watched the back of their heads, then their profiles when they turned to talk to each other. The tip of mothers nose wiggled when she talked. Father had a patch of whiskers on his jaw that he missed when he shaved. Forty-one. Forty-two. Mother was going to get groceries, then to Robinson's Stores. Fiona would go with her. It was the hardware store then the bar for Father.

Somewhere Fiona could spend the quarter father gave her for allowance. She'd been holding it since they left home. She looked at it in the centre of her palm, brought it close to her face, could smell sweat and metal together. She put it in her pocket. Sixty-three? Seventy-three? Fiona lost count.

The doctor arrived, "Lay down Fiona. We need you relaxed. I am going to hook you up to this machine. It will monitor your heart for half an hour. It'll be easier to check for abnormalities if I have a graph to read."

Fiona lay on the examining table hooked up to a machine making a graph of her heart beats. Something for the Doctor to read. She was alone in the little room. She stared at the holes in the ceiling tiles. No pattern.

Something to read. Read the heart. Sweethearts, Sweet Tarts. Be Mine. Grandpa and Grandma had heart attacks. How does something that stops attack? Attack of the Killer Heart. Broken Heart. Maybe I'll need heart surgery. Tales of the Heart. Heart Chronicles by Dr. Jean. My heart is wearing out. Loosing heart. Affairs of the Heart. That's what I need before I die.

Mother had the shopping cart half full. She walked along the aisles selecting items. Fiona followed slowly pushing the cart counting heart beats again.

"Mrs. Adams says the heart never stops even while we sleep and everything else is resting," she said to her mother.

"Uh huh," Mother said. She was holding two jars of strawberry jam, deciding which one to put in her cart.

A hundred and fifty. A hundred and fifty one.

"Can we get some of those chocolate covered cookies?" asked Fiona.

"No," mother said, "I'll make cookies this weekend."

"But Mom, you can't make them like store-bought."

Mother just looked at her and put a package of soup crackers in the cart and walked to the check-out.

Three Hundred. Three hundred and one. Fiona counted heart beats all the way through Mother paying for the groceries. Kelly's big brother was putting them in the trunk. Mother gave her another quarter. She bought two comics, a bag of chips, and a bottle of pop. Mother decided against Robinson's Stores and was going to get Father.

"Wait in the car until we get back. You can read your comic books."

Five hundred. Five hundred was enough to count.

Fiona stared at the ceiling still trying to find a pattern in the holes. The little room was quiet, all she could hear was her breathing and her heart beats if she plugged her ears.

Wonder who's in the waiting room now. Wonder why I had to take my clothes off for this. She began to bite her finger nails. Wonder what time it is now? Diagram of the ear. Hush, hush the wall has ears. Tell me, tell me what you hear. "I'll tell you all my secrets," she whispered, " but I need a heart not an ear - diagram the heart."

"Being sick is no excuse for not having the house in order in the first place," she mimicked.

What will I tell him? The doctor wanted more tests? I didn't think I'd be gone so long? The doctor was over booked? Traffic was heavy? There is something terribly wrong with me?

Fiona was waiting for mother and father. Superman had taken care of all the bad guys and Betty and Veronica were off shopping. Fiona sat with all the car doors locked, read Betty and Veronica twice, Superman once. It was a long afternoon. She watched people walk by. Counted how many ladies wore dresses, 25, and how many wore pants, 38. She waved at Shelly who was with her Mom and Brenda who was with her Grandma. Mother and father were in the Gateway Hotel...in the Beer Parlour. Fiona couldn't go in there. She tried once but a lady stopped her, said she was too young. Fiona opened the door, heard lots of people talking, glasses clinking, and then she was pulled away.

"Little girl, you can't go in there!" the woman exclaimed. She had red lipstick on. Fiona stared at the woman, then she stared at the door. The sign above it said LADIES AND ESCORTS.

"I want to get my mom,"

"I'm sure she'll be out soon, you go and wait for her where she can find you."

Fiona walked slowly back to the car. She sat in the back seat and stared at the hotel door Mother disappeared into. She remembered the smell and sounds that came out through that door. Fiona wondered what escorts were. She wondered what a beer parlour looked like inside. She thought she had heard her mother's laugh. She imagined Superman taking her home. I'd leave a note : Don't worry, Superman flew me home. See you when your finished in town. Fiona sighed and began reading Superman again.

Fiona walked in the back door.

"You're late."

Fiona looked at the man. He was washing dishes. He was very angry.

"What did you do all day? A Doctors appointment only takes half an hour, so you leave these for me to do?"

Why tell him. It wouldn't make him any less angry.

Fiona looked at him for a moment" The doctor was over booked, you didn't have to do those. I'll finish after we eat."

"I've already eaten."

"I think you just have to cut down on the stress in your life," Dr. Jean told her, " and less caffeine. I'd like you to come back next month for another check and we'll do another graph. I want to keep an eye on you."

Eyes now. Eyes and ears. Fiona sighed.

It was dark. Fiona was riding in the back seat of the car. Mother and father were in the front. The light of the dash board made shadows on their profiles as they talked and ate at the same time. They were all eating Kentucky Fried Chicken. When Mother and Father came back to the car Fiona said she had read her comic books so many times she couldn't count

them. Mother said she had so many beers she couldn't count them, so they
were having chicken for supper. Fiona put her head back and looked out
the car window at the sky. Mrs. Adams said that numbers went on for ever
and ever and never ended, and that there were too many stars to count.
Fiona found the big dipper, counted seven stars. Seven for good luck. Fiona
finished her second piece of chicken. She began counting heart beats
again. Starting at 500.

It was going to be a long night. She hugged the edge of the bed;
far enough away so she couldn't feel the anger of the man on the other
side. Two inches closer and she'd feel the cold of it, like cement floors in
winter, or a brick wall, something cold and hard she would run into if she
moved.

Remember the guy, who asked you to dance the night everyone went
to the club? The lonely fellow who asked her to have a drink in his hotel
room and left her standing on the dance floor when she said no. Suddenly
he had to pee. A quick excuse, his advance wasn't going anywhere. She had
laughed out loud.

Fiona shifted her hips and thought of her aunt. Always there were people who wanted her to do things she didn't want to do. Mother wanted
her to clean her room. The man on the other side of the bed wanted her to
keep house and have sex only once a week. Aunt Ethel wanted her to have
religion. God, Jesus, angels, miracle cures, the whole thing.

Aunt Ethel didn't approve of her name. Fiona was too frivolous, not in
keeping with the family tradition. She would have preferred Margaret or
Gretchen, something sturdy with hard consonants in it. Maria even would
have almost been outside of respectability but it was the name of the
mother of God, the name of Fiona's long suffering sainted grandmother.

How could he sleep emanating all that anger? Where did it come from?
Why was it there? But it was there all the time. Separate beds may have
been more to his liking perhaps; more comfortable for her. Actually it was
like sleeping with two people, not much left of the bed when you made
room for the anger.

Outside there was snow and winds blowing -30 all over the neighbourhood. The sky would be clear, maybe, with a show of Northern Lights. She
could get up and look.

Well, she told herself, wait a while. If she left the anger would take her
small space and there would be no room for her. Wonder what you did
wrong this time? This time, she repeated. Well, well, what else is new.

God, Jesus, the Northern Lights, Aunt Ethel. She remembered the quarter bright and shining sitting in the brass collection plate. It had red velvet
on the bottom so the quarter shone, didn't clank against metal and then

her cousin put his in too.

"Kissing cousins," he said, "that's what we are."

The two quarters in the collection plate disappeared down the row of people sitting on the same bench; passed hand to hand until it disappeared out of sight. Pews her aunt had called them. Peeeew, Fiona thought.

"We go to the Alliance Church now. The girl can stay only if she comes to church with us."

Church. That's what I did wrong, didn't go.

Robert wanted her to have religion too. She'd already had Aunt Ethel's in her youth. He didn't count it as enough. Perhaps it was the dishes though.

"Make sure you help your aunt with the dishes," Mother whispered and left.

"Peter you really should take her to Sunday School." The voice was shrill. Obviously this was neglectful on Father's part.

"You have to say your prayers dear - choose one, " Aunt Ethel was holding out a small box with coloured paper slips. This was like fortune cookies - pick a prayer before every meal.

"Say your prayers girl," she listened to her Aunt praise the heavens on high for the disappearance of her cancer. The doctors had all given up hope, a miracle cure.

" The Lord will come in a blinding flash of light and free us all from the confines of our earthly existence. Say your prayers girl, say your prayers."

Two weeks she stayed getting religion while mother and father disappeared. Two weeks and then she was home where the coyotes lived under the bed in the dark. Mommy, daddy, and baby coyotes.

Northern Lights. The first time she noticed the Northern Lights it was terror. Aunt Ethel told her Jesus would come with lights and take her away. There they were, bright lights in the sky moving, changing shape. She hadn't said her prayers, and the coyotes kept howling and the lights went away, and the curtains blew at the window.

Four thirty am. Morning indeed. She could get up, sit in front of the big window, keep the light off and watch the patterns dance above the house. Cosmic curtains blowing in the night.

"Hot milk and honey. It helps you sleep and calms the nerves. Drink it up girl."

Good idea. Fiona crawled out of bed. Moved quietly to the kitchen. She left the fridge door open to light her way while she poured milk into a cup and put it into the microwave oven.

Milk. The milky way stars that went on forever. Star light, Star bright.

Milky Way chocolate bars. Aunt Ethel gave her one once after church. A pitcher of milk spilling out yellow stars across the blue wrapper.

She stopped the microwave before it beeped. Then walked with her cup to the living room. She sat on the floor in front of the big window and pulled back the drapes. Fiona looked to the sky. Clouds. No stars, no Northern Lights. She sipped her milk, looked for lights in the houses across the street, wondering if anyone else in the neighbourhood was awake with her. A car went by, not one she recognized. Fiona let the drapes fall back into place and finished her milk in the dark. I should try to go to sleep now. Fiona stood by the edge of the bed. She wondered how he could sleep like that: flat on his back, arms folded on his chest like a dead man. He never moved. Even if he would roll on his side the anger might move too and she could have more of the bed, but he never did.

The coyotes would go away before it was daytime she told herself as she crawled into bed. And she knew as she hugged the edge of the bed, the man on the other side and his anger would both get up in the morning and finally make room for her in the bed.

Fiona lay in the tub with most of her head under water. She pushed her face to the surface so she could breath but kept her ears underwater to listen to her heartbeats. They sounded far away and echoed slightly, the same way the sound of waves echoed when you listened to ocean shells. She made waves with her hands.

That's what the visit to the doctor did, made waves. She listened hard, tried to hear something wrong and couldn't. She moved her arms and legs making waves until water sloshed over the side of the tub.

Father was pouring drinks for the search party. Mother was making bacon and eggs for their breakfast. Fiona was buttering toast listening. Brenda's dad drowned in the lake. They found his boat broken on the shore but not him. It had been storming for three days and the waves had whitecaps.

"Never go onto the lake when it looks like that," father told her once. "Especially when the water and the sky are both that colour."

Fiona looked at the sky he pointed to, looked at the water; remembered the shade of dark gray and never went close to the shore when it was that colour. She was afraid if she did, the water might vacuum her in when no one was around.

The men from the search party were talking trying to figure out why Brenda's dad went out in the boat with the weather warning in effect. No one knew. They were saying that people who drowned had their life pass before their eyes like a movie. Father sent Fiona to the basement to get another bottle of rye. No one was going to search any more. They said they probably wouldn't find him til spring if they hadn't found him by now.

Fiona tried to phone Brenda. It was a long time before she came to the phone. She told Fiona she didn't want to talk to anyone and hung up on her.

This is all wrong.

Fiona moved her arms and legs harder. The bathroom floor was covered in water. She heard a banging on the door.

"You're making a mess."

Fiona smiled to herself. "I'll clean it up," she yelled back. She took a deep breath and slid on her back until her head was under water. Twenty years later they found Brenda's father. A white skull washed up on the beach. One gold tooth intact. They identified him by dental records. She could hear a rumbling when she was underwater. He was still yelling at her. She couldn't hear what he was saying. She stayed under water until her lungs felt like bursting. Drowning. Drowning in pity. She lifted her head out of the water.

"We have an early start tomorrow." she heard him yell.

"Yeah, Yeah," she said quietly as she climbed out of the tub.

Early start. Never missed a mother's day since he left home.

Fiona mopped up the water and went to bed. His clothes for the next day were neatly organized on the chair by his side of the bed.

"Should take us seven hours and fifteen minutes - but we can only stop once - we'll make it in time for dinner and beat Billy's record."

Fiona turned out the light. A long day of driving. Beating records. I'd rather stay home.

Gas station washrooms are all the same. She thought washing her hands a second time. All smell like stale urine and cheap air freshener. She looked in the mirror. Her eyes were wide and frightened. I left my purse in the car.

"I almost left you in there," he said the last time they travelled.

"Left me?" she asked. "Why"?

"Don't know, felt like it. I had the urge to just drive away and go home without you. Maybe I will sometime."

She took her purse with her to every washroom from then on.

Fiona did not want to open the door. She was afraid the car would be gone. The man in the car did not wanted to stop. They had argued.

" Hurry up," he said. So she ran.

She stared at the door then read the walls again. Cheryl loves Lloyd July 27/92. Lloyd loves everyone Sept9/94. SM loves JR. Tanya and Sara were here July 1995.

Fiona listened to the traffic passing by. I wonder where they are all going. She stared at the door handle. I could be stranded 500 miles from home. All she had to do was open the door and see if the car was still there.

"No way of getting you home," Miss Hill said, "You'll come to my place for now, have supper with me."

Red pens. Fiona remembered Miss Hill had red pens and hit everyone on the head with them for talking. She had black shoes that clunk-clunked when she walked. Miss Hill was the tallest person Fiona ever met except for Father and the oldest person she had ever seen except for Grandma. Supper with teacher?

Fiona was nervous. They had forgotten to pick her up after school. Mother sent a note in the morning saying she was not to get on the bus. Home was 20 miles away. She said good-bye to all her grade 1 friends, watched her bus leave. She said good-bye to all the teachers, even Mr. Simpson. There was only Miss Hill, Fiona, and the janitor left at school.

What if I have to stay overnight at her house? What would Brenda and Shelly think?

What would they think now? She asked herself staring at the air freshener on the wall. She sighed. The petty things people do to try and make bad things better.

He'll be impatient now. I'm taking too long, or he's gone. I'm afraid to find out which.

" Come along Fiona," Miss Hill said shifting her shopping bag from one black gloved hand to the other. Hippity hop. Fiona had to hippity hop to keep up with her. "You'd best hold my hand child or you'll get lost." Fiona stopped hopping and walked as quickly as she could beside the woman. What if people think we're related.

Miss Hill lived in a big brick building with more stairs than the school. The floor looked the same as in Mr. Treger's store. She counted 25 steps to get to Miss Hill's bedroom. That's all her home was, a bedroom with a table and a cupboard. She made Fiona wash her hands in the washroom down the hall. The toilet had a black seat. Then there was tuna and crackers for supper.

"Please," and "Thank-you," Fiona said and did not talk much in case Miss Hill had red pens at home too.

"Tuna sandwiches." Fiona whispered. The man in the car hated tuna sandwiches. She looked at her watch. Three minutes she'd been in here. She went back to the cubicle and stared at the toilet. White with a black seat.

Miss Hill told her the neighbours were coming to get her. She didn't know how Miss Hill knew that, or how they would ever know where Miss Hill lived. Fiona looked at her. Miss Hill looked back. Fiona smiled. Miss Hill gathered the dishes. Fiona walked down the hall to help her wash them in the bathroom. Mr. and Mrs. Gray came just as they were finishing, mumbling apologies for her parents, an unexpected trip out of town.

"So sorry, communication break-down. She'll stay the night with us."

Fiona walked down the stairs. Counted 24 this time. When she was outside she looked up at the building. Miss Hill was at the window. Fiona smiled and waved. All the way home she thought of her new friend.

The next day at school Shelly was talking to her. Fiona was telling her all about where Miss Hill lived.

Miss Hill walked down the row to their desks, "There'll be no talking girls." and hit both of them on the head with her red pen.

Fiona paced. Counted eight steps wall to wall. Twenty little wee steps and four big ones. She looked at her watch. Five minutes. Long enough. She walked to the door and then turned, reached into her jacket pocket. She pulled out a tube of lipstick, a five dollar bill, and her keys. Fiona faced the wall. ROBERT JAMES IS AN ASSHOLE she wrote, looked at the wall before throwing the lipstick away. Fiona tucked the money and keys back into her pocket. She turned and walked to the door, held her breath and opened it.

The car was still there. Slowly she walked across the parking lot to the car. There was no one in the driver's seat.

Fiona walked around to the drivers side of the car, opened the door with her keys, got in and started it. She looked around, still no sign of him. Must be in the washroom. Fiona shoved the car into gear, pulled onto the highway and drove away from the washroom with the big pink letters and the sad ineffective air freshener.

Fiona looked at the clock on the dash. Four more hours and I'll be home. She started feeling hungry. Mentally she did a check list of her fridge and cupboards. Bread, mayo, onions, celery, tuna. Tuna sandwiches. Her mouth started watering. Tuna sandwiches for supper. There was beer in the fridge too, not something that Miss Hill would have on hand. Fiona smiled, pushed her foot down a little more on the gas pedal and felt like she was driving off into the sunset.

*   *   *

John Olerud and Benazir Bhuto were Fiona's heros. John Olerud because he was so human. She identified with that. Fiona always admired

the way he tried so hard to improve and get better. Just as everyone was
telling John Olerud jokes he turned into a great first baseman. She always
thought if she worked as hard at life as he did playing baseball, eventually
she would be a good person.

Benazir Bhuto was the kind of woman Fiona wanted to be. Ms. Bhuto
was a head of state in a country were religion and social norms didn't
approve of a woman in a place of power. Fiona saw her as strong, able to
voice her opinion, politically powerful, a social activist for women and children, strength in face of enormous adversity.

Fiona was sitting in a room on the eighth floor of the Hilton Hotel in
downtown Edmonton. She was drinking her second beer at the table by
the window. The bus she was supposed to be on left four hours ago. She
was here and not on the bus because she asked herself what her heros
would do in a situation like hers. She figured that John Olerud would do
something spectacular like hit a home run or catch an impossible ball and
Benazir Bhuto would make a change.

She could see the bus depot from the window. She probably had a
week before Robert cancelled the credit card. By then she would have a
place to stay and some kind of job even if it was waitressing. It didn't matter, there was just her anyway. Her life in Saskatoon was just too far away,
no point in going back because there was no way to get there not even by
bus. Mother was playing her endless games of solitaire, drinking coffee
with her friends; Robert would be puttering in the house cleaning things
that were already clean. Moving to Edmonton was like hitting a home run,
something out of the ordinary.

She had everything she needed anyway, a couple changes of clothes,
her toothbrush, and her good luck talisman.

She put her empty beer bottle on the table and fingered the dried
piece of bubble gum. It was going to be alright. She smiled watching miniature buses pull in and out of the bus depot. From this height she imagined
minature reunions and goodbyes, little people with the same tears kisses
and hugs she watched full sized not too long ago.

She put her talisman in her purse and brushed her teeth. There were
jobs in the morning paper she wanted to apply for. Which lipstick she
asked herself as she pulled out her make-up bag looking at the
names...Unlimited Rose? Perfect Petal? Very Cherry? Pink Fantasy?

One by one Fiona dropped the lipsticks into the garbage. She needed a
new colour for the occasion.

Fiona closed the drapes before she went out. Somewhere she thought,
was a miniature bus with the number 1184 travelling down the highway
with my old face still plastered against the window forever looking out.